XXX DELIGHTS

A COLLECTION OF EROTIC TALES

ANNA HEAVEN

First published in 2020 by Anna Heaven
Copyright © 2020 Anna Heaven
The right of Anna Heaven to be identified as the author of this work has been
asserted in accordance with the Copyright, Designs and Patents Act, 1988.
All rights reserved. No part of this publication may be reproduced or
transmitted in any form or by any means, electronic or mechanical, including
photocopy, recording or any information storage and retrieval system, without
permission in writing from the publisher.

ABOUT THE AUTHOR

Anna Heaven spends most of her time curled up on the sofa with her laptop.

She loves creating hot, sexy stories that give people pleasure.

When she's not working she loves sipping cocktails with friends, Salsa dancing, and creating home-cooked masterpieces.

Anna loves to hear from her readers. If you have a story you'd like her to write, or if you just want to say hi, you can contact her at authorannaheaven@gmail.com (Please, no pictures), on Twitter as @HeavenErotica, or on Facebook as AuthorAnnaHeaven.

You an also sign up for her newsletter for updates on new releases, sneak previews, and general chitchat at:

http://eepurl.com/hdUqvj

or

https://annaheavenerotica.wordpress.com/

newsletter/

WEBCAM GIRL

WEBCAM GIRL

"Hi, can you see me? Wait, let me adjust the camera. There, that's better. Hello, my name is Chantal and I'm all yours for the next hour."

I've picked my outfit, a red silk blouse and black pleated mini skirt, to be revealing, but not too revealing as it's your first time with me, and I'm positioned on the bed in a way I hope will make me look sexy but relaxed.

"I know you're paying for my time, but I want you to know that I want to be here with you."

I'm not lying when I say this. Yes, the money is a factor, I have college tuition to pay for, but there is something exciting about offering myself up to a complete stranger over a webcam, and the more I do it, the more excited it makes me.

"We're going to take things slowly, okay, baby?"

I undo a couple of buttons on my blouse and slide it off one shoulder, just to give you a taste of what you'll get later. You can already see my long, tanned legs as I stretch out on the bed, and I run my fingers suggestively across my shoulder as I look at you.

You've asked me a question, and it comes up as text on the bottom of my screen.

"What do I do? I'm a law student, which can be quite intense, so I spend my spare time on here, making you, and others like you, happy. Does that answer your question?"

I roll over onto my back and undo the rest of the buttons on my blouse, but I don't remove it, I leave it open, so you can see the front of my white lace bra while keeping the rest of me hidden.

I can tell by the look on your face that you're getting impatient, but all good things come to those who wait, so my gramma used to say, and while she'd probably chastise me for doing this, she'd agree with me taking my time with you. And besides, what good would I be doing you if I stripped naked right now and let you jack off in thirty seconds or less? You'd learn nothing about courtship and anticipation and foreplay, so yes, you will wait, or you can go pay your money to a different camgirl who doesn't give a rat's ass about what you actually need. But then again, maybe I am moving a little too slow, and I don't want you to think I'm stalling to bump up my paycheck, at least not yet.

"Would you like to see more of me?"

I turn over, crawl closer to the camera, and let my blouse slip from my shoulders. From your angle you can see my ample cleavage, and I slide one bra strap down my arm, then the other.

My bra has a front fastening to make it easier for me to take off for you, and I shiver with excitement as I run a hand from my neck to the clasp, teasing you for a moment before separating the cups and letting you see what I have for you.

There is no sound from my screen, but I can see your mouth opening and your arm moving beneath your desk in a regular rhythm. My mind fills in the sound, and I hear you breathing harshly as you rub your cock.

This is why I love my job. Watching you getting aroused by watching me is enough to ignite my own arousal, and my pussy is already fiery hot and aching to be touched, even though I've barely started.

I take my breasts in my hands and massage them, lifting them up so you can see how good they look, and pushing them together so you can imagine what it would be like if you stuck your rock-hard cock between them.

My hands are warm against my skin, and I take my nipples between my thumbs and fingers and roll and squeeze them until they stand up tall and hard. For a moment I lose myself, and my head falls back as I moan with pleasure at the sparks that are darting from my nipples all the way to my clit, and my panties are already wet even though my hand hasn't been down there yet.

I glance back at you, and you have this look of intense need that spurs me on.

"Do you want to hold my breasts in your big hands? I'd like that. And I'd love for you to take my nipples in your mouth and suck them hard as I run my hands through your hair and moan in your ear."

I rise to my knees and undo my skirt, pulling it down my

thighs so you can see my tiny lace panties. I should really keep you hanging on a bit longer, but my need is building and I can't help but touch myself through the sheer fabric.

You lean forward for a better look, and I see you slowly mouth the word 'fuck'. Do you have any idea how that makes me feel? To know that you want to see me so much that you can barely control yourself is the biggest turn-on there is, and my pussy spasms in response.

"Can you see how wet my panties are? I'm so hot for you I've soaked through them already. I can take them off if you want me to. All you have to do is transfer fifty dollars and I'll let you see just how desperate my pussy is for your attention."

I kick my skirt all the way off as I wait for the 'transfer complete' sign to pop up on the screen, but you're hesitating.

"It's okay, baby. We can keep doing what we're doing until your time runs out if you don't want me to go any further. I just thought you'd want to see just how wet I am, and how easily my fingers will slide in and out of my pussy."

I've been doing this a while and I know you won't be able to resist the thought of seeing me finger-fucking myself, at least I hope you won't be able to as I need this as much as you do, and sure enough you transfer the extra payment without any more coaxing.

"Thank you, baby. It makes me feel really special knowing that you want me. Now, I want you to imagine my mouth around that huge cock of yours, licking and sucking you while I play with myself."

Your hand movements speed up and your chest is rising and

falling quickly, and I know you'll finish before I even start at this rate, so I change my approach.

"Listen, baby. Stop what you're doing and follow my lead, okay? I really want us to come together, but you'll have to work with me."

Your arm stills, and I turn around so you can watch me pull my panties down over my ass. You catch a glimpse of my glistening pussy lips as I bend over and open my legs slightly to fully remove the fabric, and then I lie on the bed, roll over onto my back, and part my legs for you to see exactly what you're paying for.

Even though I can't see the computer from this angle, I have a mirror attached to the ceiling, out of your view, so I can still watch your reaction, and it's beautiful. You've moved so close to the screen that I can see the flecks of gold in your eyes, and the way you're rubbing your hand across your chin makes me want your hand to rub me instead.

I run one of my hands across my breasts while I move my the other between my legs. My fingers slide across my skin with ease as I run them the length of my slit, coating them with my juices. Then I reach down with my other hand and part my pussy lips. I close my eyes, and my entire body judders at the first touch of my clit.

I circle my finger slowly, and I moan loudly as a series of small spasms rip though me. I could carry this on for hours, but that would be selfish of me. After all, this is supposed to be your hour.

"I'm going to fuck myself now, and I want you to move your hand to the same rhythm as mine, so I can imagine it's you fucking me."

I slip a finger inside me, then two, then three. God, I'm so hot and wet, and I have to really concentrate to slow myself down. You are following my instructions perfectly, and it's a massive turn-on watching you keep the same rhythm going. It makes it so much easier to imaging it's your cock rather than my fingers fucking my pussy, and I can't help but increase the pace.

I lift my ass off the bed to give myself better access to my slit, and my arousal fills my nostrils as I move my fingers with increasing urgency. I smell sweet and musky and hot in a way that only sex can smell, and the friction of my fingers against my pussy walls is becoming more intense with every thrust.

I'm watching your face closely now, and I see your brow furrow slightly and your eyes narrow, and I can tell you're as close to coming as I am.

"Fuck me, baby," I scream out. "Oh, God, yes! I'm going to come. Come with me baby!"

I place my thumb over my clit and rub it as fast as I can, and pressure starts building straight away deep inside me, spreading outward to every part of my body. My breath is coming in gasps, and I can't help but cry out my pleasure as my body tips over into a powerful orgasm.

My pussy muscles clamp forcefully against my fingers, and my thighs and ass are soaked with my juices as my orgasm forces them out of me. I'm light-headed and giddy, and I can't help but giggle out loud as my orgasm subsides.

I glance at you in the mirror, and you are slumped back in your chair, and I know you came as well by the peaceful look on your face. Pride wells up inside me and I silently congratulate myself on a job well done as I turn around to look at the screen again.

"You did it, baby. That was the best orgasm I've ever had, and it was all thanks to you."

The timer has appeared in the corner of my screen, warning me that we only have a couple of minutes left, but I don't want to just cut you off without a decent goodbye. That just wouldn't be fair, would it?

"I have to go in a minute, baby, but I should clean myself up first, don't you think?"

I lift my hand to my face and run my tongue over my skin, licking my juices off until my fingers are no longer coated.

"I really hope we can do this again. Maybe this time next week?"

I know you won't have time to answer me, but the last thing I see before the service shuts down is the smile on your face, so I'm pretty sure you'll be back.

The company doesn't supply us with any client information so I don't even know your name, but I'm glad I got to spend an hour with you this evening, and I can pretty much guarantee that you'll be playing a big part in my dreams tonight.

THE REUNION

"And that's when Layla tripped over her heels, stumbled forward, and ended up with her head in the Dean's crotch!" The entire table erupted in laughter as Craig finished his story and tipped his glass toward Michael. "And on that note, I'd like to make a toast to the man who brought us all here tonight. Michael, we may not know you, but Layla thinks you're wonderful, and that's good enough for us. And thank you for paying for our flights and hotels. You are one generous guy."

The other four lifted their glasses and smiled in agreement at Michael.

"Honestly, it was nothing," Michael said, taking hold of Layla's hand. "I found a picture of you all while we were unpacking, and what better way of getting to know the woman I fell in love with than meeting her college friends." He kissed Layla on the lips then turned back to the table. "Well, you've shared quite a few stories this evening, but what was Layla really like back then?"

Layla bit her lip and glared at Marcie and Rebecca, silently warning them not to say anything, but before they could react, Asher placed a gift wrapped box on the table and slid it toward her.

"You want stories, Michael? I'm sure Layla remembers this one." He winked at Layla as she picked the box up, and she tilted her head at him, part warning, part confusion.

The box was about the size of the hip flask she used to sneak into classes, but that couldn't be what was inside as she still had it in her memory chest in the attic. She pulled on the ribbon, and as Michael put his arm around her and leaned in for a closer look, she lifted the lid off… and slammed it back on as quickly as she could.

Asher grinned at her as her face turned a burgundy color, and he raised an eye to the rest of the group. "Who here remembers graduation night?"

CHAPTER TWO

"We said we'd never talk about that," Marcie hissed at Asher, but he waved a hand to her and carried on speaking.

"It was graduation, and we all got together for drinks afterward, and one thing led to another, and the game was the outcome." He grinned at Michael as if he should know what was being talked about. Layla stood up and glared at him.

"We are not going there," she said, and turned to leave, but Michael grabbed her.

"I saw it was a rather graphic looking set of playing cards, and I'd love to hear where this is going," he said, and gave her hand a squeeze.

Layla sat back down and stared at him. This was a side of her he had no idea about and she was afraid that he wouldn't like what he heard, but it was too late now as everyone else inched forward around the table to talk.

"Layla came up with the idea. I mean, we'd all been close

anyway, but this took it to a whole new level." Asher looked around the table and continued. "She pulled out this deck of cards, and it started off like any other drunken game of strip poker, although the clothes came off a bit quicker. But then, once there were no more clothes to bet with, the winner got to choose who performed what sexual act with who, and you can imagine the rest."

Rebecca giggled and elbowed Marcie in the ribs. "That was the first time I… you know… so it's kind of our anniversary when you think about it."

Craig picked up where Asher left off. "It was a fucking orgy is what it was, and it was one of the best nights of my life."

Michael looked at Layla. "Well, aren't you a dark horse? Why haven't I heard about this before?"

"It was a one-time thing, and I didn't think it was worth bringing up." Layla picked up her wine glass and downed the contents.

"Are you embarrassed by it?" Michael stroked her hand and smiled.

"No, well, maybe. I mean it was college stuff, and we all let loose back then, didn't we?"

"I guess, but this… and you were the one who came up with it? I'm surprised."

The waiter appeared and began picking up the last of the plates from the table, and Layla asked for directions to the bathroom. He motioned to the back of the restaurant before continuing to clear the plates. "Can I get you anything else?" he said, "I think we still have coffee available."

CHAPTER THREE

"Shit, shit, shit," Layla said to the bathroom mirror. She took a deep breath and ran her fingers through her hair. She thought that part of her life was over and done with. The wild parties, the hook-ups, the complete disregard for social rules were all in her past, until she'd walked into the restaurant tonight.

What she'd been expecting was a quite table in the corner, set for two, with candles, roses, champagne, and a man who saw her for the mature, sophisticated woman she was, so when she turned the corner and her past stood in unison to greet her, to say it was a shock is as big an understatement as there is.

She'd fought all evening not to be drawn into reminiscing, instead trying to keep the conversation on current events, and now Michael knew that she was the type of woman to open her legs for the spin of a bottle or the deal of a hand of cards.

She thought she'd hit the jackpot when she met him. He was handsome and rich, and he was a genuinely nice guy even though he was a bit on the boring side, and she did love him.

But he was the sort of straight-laced guy who would never think of screwing someone on the first date, let alone get involved with sex parties, so what was this revelation going to do to their relationship?

She reached into her bag and pulled her lipstick out. Maintaining the appearance of being happy and in control seemed the only thing she could do, but her hand shook slightly as she applied the color to her lips.

Another deep breath in and out, and a whispered mantra of 'He loves you' three times in the mirror, and Layla pasted a smile back on her face, opened the bathroom door, and made her way back to the table.

"There you are," Michael said. "I hope you don't mind, but I mentioned we have a case of the latest Sauvignon Blanc from our family vineyard, and your friends are joining us for drinks." He smiled as he spoke, and there was a sparkle in his eyes that she hadn't seen since they first started dating.

The car journey home was excruciatingly slow, and because Michael had insisted on Layla riding in the second car to direct them home, she couldn't even question why he'd suddenly decided to invite them back. Knowing him, it was highly likely he was simply being hospitable—after all, they had flown in from all across the country, and it would have been rude to spend nothing more than a couple of hours over dinner with them—but the smile he'd given her as they left was more suggestive than happy, and it worried her.

"Gas station!" Asher leaned forward and tapped the driver on the shoulder. "Can we pull in? I need to grab a pack of smokes." The car pulled in to the parking lot and Asher jumped out. "Does anyone else want anything? Nope, okay. Be right back."

"Family vineyard, eh. You've really landed on your feet, Cass." Craig grinned and gave Layla a gentle punch to the shoulder.

"It's Michael's grandfather's vineyard in Italy. His sister runs it and we get a few cases a year as a family perk. That's all." Layla stared at the back of the driver's seat for a moment. "Look, Craig. What we were like in college… that's not me anymore, and it's certainly not Michael. I don't know why he invited you back." She shook her head. "I mean, I'm glad you're here, don't get me wrong, but…"

"He invited us back because we're your friends. And I wouldn't be so sure about Michael. He comes across as conventional, but maybe that's because it's what he thinks you want rather than who he is."

"Why would you think that? Did he say something when I was in the bathroom?"

The door opened and Asher pushed his way between them and slumped onto the seat. "Okay, let's go."

The rest of the journey consisted of Asher talking non-stop about his exes and how he was 'so done with the LA scene' while lamenting being single and missing LA at the same time, and by the time they pulled into the driveway of the house, Layla was no clearer about what Craig has said about Michael.

CHAPTER FIVE

"Wow, this place is amazing, Michael!" Rebecca wandered from the entrance hall to the dining room and into the kitchen area before finding herself in a vast living room with a glass wall overlooking a pool area.

"Wait, Michael Massey. Massey Shipping? The Fortune five hundred Masseys?" Marcie appeared behind them and threw herself down on a sofa that would sit at least six people.

Michael sat on the opposite sofa. "Yes, although I'm not directly involved with the business. I have my own software development company which keeps me busy." He leaned forward. "I have to admit it was a bit of a shock to hear about what she was like back then. That isn't the Layla I know at all."

"Yeah, she has become much more conservative recently. Don't take offence, but I thought it was because she'd met some boring, stick in the mud guy, but that doesn't seem to be the case."

"The impression I got when I met her was that she was

already conservative, and I thought that's what she wanted from me. Maybe I was wrong."

Rebecca walked up behind him, threw her arms around his shoulders, and bent down to whisper in his ear. "Maybe we can bring her back out of her shell tonight, if you're genuinely up for it."

The sound of gravel crunching under car tires indicated the arrival of Layla, Craig and Asher, and Michael moved Rebecca's arms and stood up. "Glass of wine, ladies?" He made his way to the kitchen and opened a hatch in the floor that led to a circular wine cellar as Layla led the remainder of their guests inside.

By the time the men had toured the downstairs, there were half a dozen crystal wine glasses and three bottles sitting on a tray in front of the large living room fireplace, and Michael was setting the sound system to play some background classical music.

Layla played the hostess and opened a bottle of wine, sharing it equally between the six glasses and handing one to each of their friends. Michael took the final glass, made his way to the seating area, and held his drink in the air.

"A toast. To my talented sister for her exquisite wine-making skills, and to friends, old and new." He waited for everyone to clink glasses and take a sip before adding, "And now, shall we get the cards out?"

Layla gave Michael a warning look, but he ignored her and reached into her bag for the box that Craig had given her. She grabbed her bag away from him and smiled at her guests. "Michael, can I have a word with you in private?"

He followed her into the hall way with a cheeky smile on his face, and she placed her hands on her hips and glared at him.

"What on earth are you doing? This isn't you, and it's not me anymore."

"Are you sure about that? Just spending a few hours with your friends has made it clear you were far more adventurous before we met, and maybe I was too. I think we both turned into the person we thought the other wanted without actually finding out what that was."

Layla laced her fingers together and stared at her hands. "Maybe you're right, but I'm scared, Mike. I'm scared that you'll see another side to me and you won't like it."

Michael took a step forward and kissed her, his tongue

probing her mouth, and she wrapped her arms around his waist. When they finally came up for air, he kissed the tip of her nose.

"There is nothing about you I wouldn't like. How could there be? And I think maybe we need this."

She stared into his eyes, unsure of how to answer him, but when his cheeky grin returned, she shook her head and grabbed his hand. "Fine." And as they walked back into the living room, Layla grabbed the pack of cards and threw them to Craig. "Deal, before I change my mind."

Michael lit the large fire and topped up everyone's glasses as the cards were being dealt, and he took his seat and picked his hand up. It wasn't great, with two sixes and little else, but this was the first game of poker he'd played where he was actually hoping to lose, and he suspected that everyone else around the table was thinking the same way. When it was his turn, he threw a two down and picked up his replacement, and his hand remained the same as it had been.

Five minutes later, all bar one of them had removed an item of clothing, and Rebecca was dealing a new hand and begging them to beat her on the next round. Another ten minutes, and all of them were reduced to their underwear. The wine was working its magic, and the initial embarrassment and apprehension felt by Layla had turned to excitement.

"Ladies, you know how it works." Asher grinned at them. "You don't get to claim two turns just because you have bras and panties whereas we only have a single piece of underwear."

The cards were dealt and hands were played, and Marcie looked visibly disappointed when she won. "Screw it," she said. "I'm not going to be the only one sitting here with clothes on."

Layla looked at Michael, and he gave her a wink as he stood and slipped his boxers down to his ankles. His large, thick cock stood proud and tall, and she ran her hand over its length before reaching behind her, unhooking her bra, and letting it fall to the floor, followed by her panties. Michael grabbed her breasts in both hands and ran his thumbs over her nipples, and she inhaled sharply at his touch.

"Come on you two. Play the game." Asher sat on the sofa with his erect cock in his hand, watching the display. "You only get to touch each other if directed to."

Rebecca stood and removed her underwear, her large breasts swinging as she leaned over to pull her panties off. Her pussy was clean-shaven, and her excitement showed as her juices glistened on her outer lips. Marcie reached out to touch it, but pulled her hand back and giggled at the last minute, instead quickly removing her own underwear before anyone could chastise her for breaking the rules.

Craig was the last one to stand, waiting until everyone else had undressed before taking his turn so all eyes would be on him. His tight-fitting briefs showed his erection, but it was only when he removed them and his cock sprang free that his piercings were shown. He had metal bars fitted all the way down the length of his cock, so the small balls on the end created a pattern not unlike a high-end vibrator, and four balls stood up on the tip of his cock.

"The one on the end is called a magic cross," he said, grinning, "and trust me, magic is exactly the right word. With this bad boy inside you, you'll swear all your Christmas's have come at once."

Layla couldn't take her eyes off the piercings, and her pussy pulsed at the thought of having them inside her. Then guilt flooded her and she grabbed hold of Michael's hand and squeezed it. He squeezed back to reassure her, and whispered in her ear, "this is going to be interesting."

"And… whose deal is it?" Asher glanced around the room, and Marcie picked up the pack and started shuffling the cards.

CHAPTER SEVEN

For the first time since they'd started playing, there was a good reason to want to win, and Michael held his breath as he swapped two cards, trying to will a winning hand, but it was Craig and his full house that took the game.

"Hmmmm. Can we clear the table? Rebecca, your pussy is looking very inviting, so I'd like you to lie down on your back while Marcie gives you oral. And Marcie, you don't get to stop until you make Rebecca come."

With the wine glasses removed to the floor, Rebecca took her position, and Asher shifted seats for a better view as Marcie dropped to her knees between Rebecca's thighs. She pushed Rebecca's legs as wide apart as they would go, and Michael's breathing became heavier as he leaned forward to watch.

Rebecca stretched her arms above her head and closed her eyes, and her skin erupted in gooseflesh in anticipation of the first touch of Marcie's tongue. Her smooth pussy was already soaked with juices, and every fold glistened and shone as

Marcie used her thumbs to part the outer lips to give better access to her clit.

It wasn't long before Rebecca was moaning and panting as Marcie's expert tongue circled her clit and lapped at her opening, and her flushed skin hinted that her orgasm was nearing. She reached out a hand to Layla and pulled her from the sofa, and Layla sank to the floor beside her and kissed her.

With Layla's tongue swirling around her mouth and Marcie's tongue swirling around her clit, Rebecca could no longer contain the orgasm building inside her. She screamed into Layla's mouth as her inner muscles threatened to rip themselves apart over and over, and her juices flowed from her, soaking Marcie's face and hair. Marcie continued to lick and suck at her clit until the screaming subsided into begging for her to stop, and then she licked around her pussy lips and opening, gorging herself on Rebecca's sweet taste.

When both Marcie and Layla finally sat back, Rebecca stayed where she was on the table. Her stomach rippled as the afterglow of her orgasm caused her muscles to spasm gently, her skin was flushed and glistening with sweat, and her breasts rose and fell as she focused on bringing her breathing back to normal. Once she'd managed to regain control of her body, she began to giggle uncontrollably.

"So, Michael," Craig said. "Are you enjoying the game so far?"

Michael ran his hand over Layla's thigh and smiled. "I think I am, now deal."

The next hand was a close call, with Michael sitting smugly with three jacks only to be taken down by Rebecca with three queens. She made a whooping sound as she placed her cards down and stared at Michael.

"It's time to break you in, new boy, and I'm wondering if you'll actually be up for the challenge."

"Try me." Michael leaned forward and grinned at her. "Although, as the winner, you won't get to taste this body."

Rebecca matched his body language and stared him straight in the eyes. "No, I won't, but I'm betting Asher's been hoping to get a feel of that impressive cock of yours. Ever fucked a man before?"

Layla glared at Rebecca and turned to Michael. "You don't have to do this if you don't want to, you know. It's only a game."

"You think I'd balk at the idea of fucking a man? You're forgetting I spent my teenage years at an all-boys private boarding school." He didn't wait for Layla to respond and instead turned to Asher. "Did you get the condoms?"

Asher reached into his jacket pocket and pulled out the box. "What?" he said as Layla gave him a questioning look. "You didn't honestly think I was buying cigarettes, did you? When have you ever known me to smoke?" He threw the box to Michael and took a sip of his wine, and then added, "I figured at least one of us would need some lube as well, so catch." He tossed the plastic tube and grinned.

Asher stood and winked at Michael. "Are you a quickie kind of guy or do you prefer a little foreplay?" He moved around the table to the rug in front of the fire, and when Michael approached, he pulled him in for a kiss while running a hand down his torso to stroke his cock.

Michael groaned at the feeling of a hand massaging his cock, and he slipped his tongue into Asher's mouth while gripping his ass and pulling him closer. It had been a long time since he'd felt the naked body of a male pressed against his own, and he'd forgotten how much of a turn-on it was. Asher's body was lean but muscular, and his cock pulsed against Michael's stomach, desperate for attention. It was enough to spur Michael into action, and he pulled away, ripped open a condom packet, and rolled the rubber into place.

Marcie shifted seats and grabbed Layla's hand. "So, you didn't know about his private school past I take it. How does that make you feel?"

"Confused, and oddly aroused. Knowing that he's had sex with men, he's not the person I thought I knew, but finding out that he's far more adventurous than I'd ever thought he could be, well, that opens up a whole string of possibilities."

"Yeah, I've a feeling you two are going to have a lot to talk about after this evening."

Asher's loud moan drew their attention back to the scene playing out in front of them. He was on his hands and knees, and Michael was thrusting in and out of his ass slowly. Lubricant glistened on Asher's ass cheeks, and his muscles were taut as he pushed back against Michael's hips. Michael reached around and took Asher's cock in his hand, and he started stroking it at double pace to his thrusts.

"Ah, fuck, man, I'm going to come." Asher spoke through gritted teeth, and Michael tightened his grip and increased his thrusts. "Your rug. I don't want to…"

"That's what dry cleaners are for." Michael slapped Asher's ass, his breathing ragged.

"Ahh, fuck!" Asher came, his cock spurting cum all over the rug and Michael's hand, but Michael didn't stop thrusting into him. He increased his pace even more and grabbed hold of Asher's hips, holding him up as he pounded into him. Where Asher swore when he came, Michael roared, and he held Asher's ass against him as tight as he could as his cock pulsed and spewed cum into the condom he was wearing.

Both of them sank to the floor, and Michael withdrew his cock and held Asher in a tight embrace, kissing his back and shoulders.

"I think now would be a good time to refill our glasses," Craig said, and he grabbed the last remaining bottle of wine and twisted off the lid.

CHAPTER NINE

The next hand of poker was a bit more subdued. The wine was taking effect, and both Asher and Michael were sitting back in tired relaxation after their mutual ejaculations. Michael almost missed the near flush he was holding, and initially waved Rebecca off when she asked if he wanted to change any cards, before changing his mind and sliding a card across the table. The replacement completed the flush, and he spread the cards out and grinned at the group.

"I'm guessing this means it's my turn to choose?" The rest of them threw their cards down and sat back, waiting to hear what he had to say. "When I met you, Layla, I couldn't imagine you being with anyone else. I mean, I get a twinge of jealousy if a waiter pays you too much attention. But when I saw your reaction to Craig's piercings, instead of getting jealous, I got excited. I wanted you to be able to feel what it would be like to have those piercings inside you. So that's my choice. I want Craig to fuck you, and I want to look into your eyes as he makes you come."

For a split second, Layla wanted to say no. It was all too

weird. But Michael had fucked Asher without a second thought, so why shouldn't she fuck Craig. They were already past the point of no return when it came to their relationship, and it was either going to make or break them come tomorrow. She kissed Michael and whispered, "I love you," and then she got up from her seat and held out a hand to Craig.

"Which way do you want me?" he said as he ran a hand over her breasts.

"Hmmm," she took hold of his cock and squeezed gently, feeling the metal balls against her palm. "Lie on your back in front of the fire."

He took his position and placed his hands behind his head.

"No, face the other way so I can look at Michael."

He shuffled himself around, and she straddled him and leaned down to kiss his mouth. The tip of his cock pressed against her opening, and she lifted herself up away from it.

"Not without a condom," she said, and she ripped open the wrapper, placed the contents between her lips, and shifted down his body.

The metal balls made it more difficult to maneuver the condom onto his cock, but she used her lips and tongue to ease the latex around them and into place. Craig was moaning quietly and raising his hips to meet her mouth, but Layla knew if she carried on he wouldn't be able to control himself, and she was determined to get her own needs taken care of first.

Her pussy was already wet and desperate for attention, and she repositioned herself over his cock and lowered herself onto him.

It was like nothing she'd felt before, and she closed her eyes to fully focus on her pussy. His cock was thick and long, and filled her completely, and the metal balls rubbed against her inner walls, stimulating her g-spot as she rode him. He raised his hands to her breasts as they bounced in time with her movements, and she leaned forward slightly, bringing them closer to him.

Layla rode Craig slowly, the heat in her pussy spreading outward and intensifying with each downward motion. There was no way she'd be able to keep from orgasming unless she slowed down even more, but that would mean losing the feeling of his pierced cock grinding against her inner walls, and it felt so good she wasn't about to give it up.

She remembered the rest of Michael's request and opened her eyes to look at him. He was staring at her, his eyes dark, and he had his cock in his hand, rubbing it as he watched. The sight of him, hot and horny for her fucking another guy, sent her body past the point of no return, and the heat in her pussy turned to delicious pressure.

Her breathing became ragged and her mind swam as she rode Craig's cock, and she raised her hands and knotted them through her hair as her orgasm neared. When she finally came, it was like nothing she'd experienced before. The stimulation to her g-spot created a deep, intense pleasure that moved through her inner core like a tsunami, while the rest of her body exploded into a series of spasms and convulsions.

She maintained eye contact with Michael, through the stars and fireworks, through the tears that flooded her face, and she mouthed 'I love you' over and over, although the sounds of the words were lost in a mess of moans and whimpers.

Craig grabbed hold of her hips and started thrusting himself into her as fast as he could, and before her orgasm had fully subsided, he was scrunching his face and swearing into the air as he came inside her.

Layla crawled from on top of Craig and lay down next to him, not trusting her muscles to hold her up, and she stared at the ceiling as she tried to regain control of her body.

"I hate to interrupt you," Asher held his cell phone in the air, "but I have to be at the airport in six hours and I could really do with an hour or two sleep. Would you hate me if I suggested we call it a night?"

CHAPTER TEN

Michael called a car for them while everyone sorted out their clothes and belongings, and when their ride arrived, there were lingering hugs and kisses all around.

"Let me know what happens, okay?" Marcie whispered into Layla's ear.

"Same time next year?" Asher said to Michael. "And maybe I'll get to be top."

"Maybe," Michael replied. "Although I do like being in charge."

Layla pushed them through the door and wrapped her arms around Michael as they all said their final goodbyes, and once they were safely in the car, she turned to walk back to the living room.

"Where are you going?" Michael grabbed her by the hand.

"I was just going to clean up a bit."

"Leave it and come to bed. We'll do it in the morning."

She shrugged and followed him up the stairs. She was dog tired, but she doubted she could sleep given the events of the evening, and she didn't really want to discuss the evening with Michael until she'd had a chance to think it over first.

He led her to the bed and lifted the covers so she could get in, and then he slid in next to her and nuzzled his face against her neck.

"Tonight was definitely an eye-opener, and it was a lot of fun, but—"

She stopped him. "Don't, please. Not now. I know things have changed between us, and when we wake up tomorrow, they'll never be the same, but I want to take tonight to believe we'll be okay."

"Wait, what?" He sat up and looked at her. "You think we won't be okay?" He leaned forward, took her face in his hands, and kissed her slowly. "Yes, things have changed, but the thing I took from this evening most of all is that I want you." He kissed the side of her neck. "I want all of you, and while it would be great to be more adventurous," his lips brushed the top of her breasts, "what I love more than anything is being here with you," he ran his tongue down her stomach, "just you, like this."

His mouth found her mound, and he pulled her pussy lips apart, giving him access to her clit. She moaned and ran her hand through his hair as he licked and sucked at her most sensitive part, and when she was close to coming, he kissed back up her body and slowly thrust his cock inside her as his lips found her mouth.

He was right, Layla thought. Craig and his piercings may have been a great fuck, but having Michael inside her made her feel whole, and no matter what happened after this evening, she would never want to be without him again.

THE HOUSE MATE

CHAPTER ONE

It was almost midnight as I pulled the car up into my designated parking space. The lights were on in our ground floor apartment which meant that Rob was home. Damn it. After being away for the last six months on a working holiday to Australia I was at least hoping for a few hours of peace to unpack and shower.

He was usually at work at this time, night shifts in the ER paid better than day shifts, and his rota had been the same for the five years we've lived together as roommates. That suited me perfectly, as although I liked him, his incessant chattering got on my last nerve, and our opposing work schedules meant we only spent a few hours at most together.

But he was here, and I couldn't sit in the car all night, so I got out of the driver's seat, opened the boot and started pulling out my luggage. My back was turned and my head was wedged inside the trunk as I tried to wrestle a large suitcase that had managed to get itself stuck, so I didn't hear him approaching.

"Chelsea!" I lost my footing and almost ended tits-up in the trunk, but he caught me around the waist and pulled me back. "Why didn't you call when you landed? Here, let me get that." He seemed oblivious to the fact that he'd almost given me a heart attack and started jabbering on about some patient or other he'd had to wheel half way around the hospital last week while he unhooked my suitcase from the trunk.

He brushed against me as placed the suitcase on the ground and my stomach did a little whirl. What the hell was that? I'd never been attracted to Rob, he simply wasn't my type, so why was my body suddenly reacting to him? It had to be the aftershave he was wearing. I hadn't noticed anything like that about him before so this must be a new brand. It was a warm musk, with slight earthy undertones and just a hint of citrus, or that's the only way I could think of describing it. Whatever it was it was certainly having an effect on me.

As Rob helped me get my stuff into the apartment I considered asking him about it, but that was probably better left for another time. He could have changed it for a new woman in his life, and asking him would lead to every single detail being shared when all I wanted to do was sleep. No, whatever was going on with him could wait until another day.

Once inside, Rob headed for the kitchen. "Fancy a coffee?" he called, "I'm dying to hear all about your trip."

"Do you mind if I head straight to bed?" I called back. "I haven't slept in nearly forty-eight hours and my eyelids are hitting the floor."

"No, of course not. We'll catch up tomorrow though, yeah?"

"Yes, tomorrow is good. Night, Rob," I said, and I headed into the bedroom.

CHAPTER TWO

It was pitch black, and I felt around with both hands, trying to get my bearings. My left hand hit something hard and I ran my fingers over it. Bark. I was in a wood or a forest, but how? A branch snapped somewhere behind me, then again, louder this time, slightly to my right. Whatever was with me was getting closer.

I held my breath, trying to listen for the smallest of sounds. I should have been scared, but I wasn't. I was excited. Suddenly, I felt warm breath on the back of my neck, and smelled that strange masculine muskiness. I knew it was Rob, but at the same time it wasn't.

He pushed me up against the tree so the bark scratched my face, and his hands tore at my clothes, shredding them. My top fell away first, followed by my skirt, and then my panties. "You're mine, bitch. You've always been mine," he said, as he leaned in and sniffed my hair and neck. "I've waited long enough, and now I'm going to take what's mine."

I held on to the tree trunk as his hands reached around and

grabbed my breasts. His palms were hot against my skin, and his nails were long and sharp. As his body pressed against me, I could feel course hair covering his torso, and I bit my lip as he pulled my hips toward him and positioned himself at my entrance.

He thrust in to me with urgency, and I moved my hips to his rhythm, desperate to get more of him even though he was filling me completely. He was growling in my ear, and his teeth grazed along my neck as he pounded into me from behind. Delicious tension was building in my core, and I wanted him to fuck me harder, faster, to rip me apart with his nails, to sink his teeth deep into my flesh… and then I was coming, my muscles straining against his massive manhood as they spasmed with pleasure. I threw my head back and howled at the sky, and when he came, we howled in unison.

CHAPTER THREE

S hit, fuck! I sat up in bed, panting hard. What the hell was that? It had to be the jet lag screwing with my brain, surely? I had never had a dream that visceral before. Even my wet dreams where I woke up still shuddering from an orgasm faded quickly when I realized I was awake. This was something different, and it kind of scared me.

I sat on the side of the bed and pulled a robe around me before making my way through to the kitchen and filling the coffee machine. There was no sign of Rob, so he was either still in bed or on a day shift, but his scent lingered in the air. I tried to shake it off, but it kept drawing me back to the dream, so once the machine started burping and spluttering, I made my way around our shared area and opened all the windows wide.

The morning sky was clear, and I sat with my coffee watching a cheeky pine squirrel darting in and out of the trees and onto the grass verge on the other side of the courtyard. Slowly, my mind cleared, and the dream was all but forgotten as I made a mental list of the things I needed to get done.

Laundry was the most urgent chore, as I'd purposely not washed any of my clothes for over two weeks because I knew I'd have to pack them all together in my suitcase anyway. I did have a couple of tshirts and sweatpants in my wardrobe that would be fine for now, but I wouldn't be seen dead wearing those outside. I also needed to give my manager a call to let her know I was back in the country and available for work. I'd been paid a decent amount for the Australian contract, but being a model takes work and money, and I needed to find another job sooner rather than later. Finally, I needed to book hair, nail, and waxing appointments with my regular cosmetologists as I'd really missed being able to relax and let them work their magic knowing that I'd get exactly the outcome I wanted.

I finished my coffee and headed into the bedroom to throw some clothes on. Once I was dressed, I tied my hair back and emptied the contents of my suitcase into a washing basket. The washer was in a small utility room to the side of the kitchen, and as I opened the door I was hit with the smell of Rob again. He'd left a basket of his clothes on the counter top, and I tried my best to ignore it as I filled the machine, popped in some detergent, and turned it on.

The washer was temperamental, so I leaned against the wall, planning on waiting until the wash cycle kicked in before getting on with my other chores. God, Rob's smell was so good, and I closed my eyes for a moment as I breathed it in. The next thing I knew, I had a pair of his boxers pushed up against my nose and a hand down the front of my sweatpants. My head was spinning with the thought of him pinning me to the wall and pulling my pants down as my fingers worked against my clit as fast as they could.

I knew exactly what I was doing, but it was as if I had no control over my body. My panties were already soaked through, and my fingers slid against my clit and into my opening as I groaned and panted. I pushed his boxers tighter against my face as pressure grew within my body, and my arms and legs shook as I finger-fucked myself into a mind-blowing orgasm.

My body was still spasming as I sank to the floor and wrapped my arms around myself. What the hell was happening to me? I knew I needed to speak to Rob, but at the same time, the thought of seeing him at the moment filled me with both longing and dread. Was it simply the new after-shave he was wearing, or had something about him changed to make me lust after him like this? Or had I changed in some way that I was unaware of? Maybe I was sick, delirious, or something was affecting my senses, sending them into over-drive. I scrambled up from the floor and ran to the bathroom, where I turned the shower on as cold as I could bare and stood underneath the spray until my body and mind went numb.

CHAPTER FOUR

The slam of the front door brought me back to reality, and I hauled my shivering body from the shower and wrapped myself up in a towel. How was I going to approach this? Even though it had to happen, this was going to be one of the most awkward conversations we'd had, and I really hoped it didn't affect our living arrangements.

He was in his room getting changed, so I ran to the bedroom and threw on the ugliest clothes I could find, and then I made my way out to the living room and sat on the sofa, waiting for him. Finally, he wandered into the kitchen and popped the kettle on the stove.

"I picked up some Chai at the market. Do you fancy a cup?" he shouted as he clattered around.

"Thanks, yeah," I said. I didn't really want one, but it would make things less uncomfortable. The kettle squealed, and two minutes later Rob placed two mugs down on the coffee table and flopped onto the other end of the sofa.

"So, are you going to tell me your news or do you want to

hear mine first?" he said. I figured that his news might give me some insight into what had changed, and I didn't trust myself to speak straight away as his scent was beginning to overwhelm me again. "I quit my job, finally. That crazy patient I was telling you about last night attacked me, and I'm fine, but it made me reevaluate things. It was the right move, and I'm feeling so much more confidence than I used to."

I grabbed my mug and held it up close to my nose to help mask his smell. "So there isn't a new woman on the scene?"

Rob laughed. "What makes you say that?"

"I don't know. You've been wearing a new aftershave or deodorant, and I figured it was for a woman." I glanced at him over the steam from the tea, and I could see that it wasn't just the scent. He looked different; healthier, fitter, more muscular.

"I haven't changed my products," he said. "Maybe you just forgot what they smelled like. You have been away for six months, don't forget."

"Are you sure? It's definitely different."

"Absolutely sure. What's going on, Chelsea? You seem on edge. As if you don't want to be here with me." He leaned forward, his eyes studying my face, and I could see every ripple of his muscles as he moved… and I wanted to reach out and touch him so badly.

"I don't know. Maybe it's jetlag, but you're different somehow. And I dreamt about you last night; a weird, crazy, messed up dream."

I coughed and got up from the sofa to increase the space between us. My brain was working overtime trying to find a way to explain what was happening that wouldn't make me sound like I was having some sort of mental breakdown. Rob stood up and moved toward me, and I held out my arm to stop him getting any closer.

"You smell different, and it's… umm… I'm not saying it's you, but your smell is… oh God, it's turning me on, okay?" I could feel the heat raging through my cheeks as I spoke, and I glanced around the room, desperately looking for something to focus on that wasn't him. "I don't want to ruin what we have because my brain is playing tricks on me, but it's scaring me because I don't know what's happening."

He brushed my arm away and stood inches away from my face. My body was tingling with desire, and I could feel my juices running down the inside of my thighs, and I tried, desperately, to turn away, but all I wanted to do was throw myself at him.

"I don't want to ruin our relationship either, but you have to know how hard it's been for me living here with you. I have always been attracted to you, Chelsea, and I don't know what is happening right now, but would it be so bad if we gave in to it?"

CHAPTER FIVE

His breath was hot against my face, and I tried to fight against what I was feeling, but this animalistic need inside me was too hard to ignore, and I grabbed his face and thrust my tongue into his mouth as my hands reached under his shirt and clawed at his chest.

He groaned into my mouth and grabbed my ass, lifting my legs so I could wrap them around him. His teeth grazed across my neck, and I gasped for air until his mouth clamped down on mine again as he carried me to his bedroom.

I landed on the bed with a thump, and he crawled over me, his eyes filled with desire. I stared back at him as I yanked my sweats and panties down, not caring any more where these sudden urges were coming from and simply wanting to feel him inside me as quickly as possible. He had other ideas.

Rob grabbed the hem of my tshirt and pulled it over my head, then he pushed me back down, took a handful of my hair, and inhaled deeply. He groaned against my ear as he did so, before licking at my earlobe, neck, shoulder, chest, and stopping to focus on my breasts. He took them in his hands and squeezed them, his thumbs running across my nipples, and he grinned at me before lowering his head and sucking each one in turn.

I was already writhing with desire as his head move further down my body, and he stopped when he reached my pussy, using his fingers to hold my labia apart, giving him full access to my clit. Excitement was already building inside me at what was about to happen, but he didn't move, and even when I raised my hips invitingly, he stayed just out of contact. Suddenly, I could feel cold air brushing my clit as he took a deep breath in, and when he exhaled, heat washed over me. It was such an intense feeling I had to close my eyes and concentrate to stop myself tipping over the edge, and it seemed to go on forever, but then his tongue lapped from my opening to my clit, and my body exploded.

He crawled up my body and positioned his cock at my open-ing, and then he very slowly pushed inside me. My body opened up to him, and I grabbed fistfuls of his hair, pulling his face to mine. In that moment, I forgot all my misgivings and gave myself to him completely as he filled me. I breathed him in, filled my mouth with his taste, and my pussy with his long hard cock, and as he fucked me, I felt owned, and loved, and needed.

My body rumbled toward a deeper orgasm as his thrusts quickened, and he didn't slow his pace as I shuddered beneath him. When tears burst from my eyes, he licked them away, and groaned against my cheek, his need for me as much as mine for him. I seemed to be caught in a constant orgasm, with a new one building before the last one subsided, and when he finally came, roaring in my ear, I roared with him.

We lay there in each other's arms, soaked in sweat and body fluids, and once Rob got his breath back, he turned to look at me.

"You said something about a dream earlier. What was it?"

I lifted my hand and teased damp hair from his forehead. "It was nothing. As I said, probably just jetlag."

"The thing is…" he turned his gaze to the ceiling and paused for a moment. "No, tell me about your dream first. I want to know what's inside that mind of yours."

"Okay, but don't laugh," I said, and I sat up and pulled the sheets around my body. He did laugh at those words, but then he apologized and motioned for me to carry on. "I was in the woods and it was dark. You were there, only it wasn't *you* you."

"What do you mean?" he said, the smirk that had been on his face disappearing.

"It was more like a wild animal, but it had your smell… your new smell, and rather than being afraid, I was excited by it."

He sat up next to me, his forehead furrowed, and he played with his knuckles, avoiding eye contact. "I've had the same dream. For the past week I've had these dreams about running through trees, but last night you were there with me, and I was hunting you. Only it wasn't to hurt you… And I woke up covered in dirt. I don't know what the hell is going on, Chels."

I was struggling to process what he was telling me. How was it possible for us to have the same dream? Something was going on, and whatever was happening was affecting the both of us. I should probably have packed an overnight bag and gone to stay with friends for a few days to figure everything out, but I didn't want to leave Rob. The feelings I had for him might have been connected to the dreams, but they were overpowering, and I needed to be with him, to help and protect him, and to kiss him and hold him and fuck him… Shit, why couldn't I stop thinking about him for even a second?

"Maybe you're sleepwalking," I said. "I could stay here with you tonight and keep an eye on you, and I know I'm not supposed to wake you if you are sleepwalking, but I could at least follow you to make sure you don't hurt yourself." I stood up and wrapped the sheet around my body. "Maybe I was dreaming because I picked up on a vibe from you that something was wrong. That makes sense, right?"

"I guess," he said, lying back down and watching me as I made my way to the door. I poured myself a glass of water, and another for Rob, and I carried them back to the bedroom before heading to my own room to grab a clean pair of sweatpants and a top. If this was a case of him sleepwalking, I had to be prepared to go after him, and I didn't want to risk wasting time finding something to wear and losing him. My running shoes were in the corner and I picked them up before turning the light out. It would be strange spending the night with Rob, but no stranger than the past twenty-four hours, and I was kind of looking forward to getting to know him more intimately.

CHAPTER SIX

B y the time I got back to his room, I was brimming with questions I wanted to ask him, but his gentle snoring told me he was already asleep. Oh well, there was always tomorrow. I placed my stuff on top of a chest of drawers and climbed into bed, and as soon as I'd pulled the covers over myself, he turned over and curled up against me.

My head was swirling with thoughts as I lay next to him, and it wasn't long before I was drifting off to sleep. Suddenly, Rob sat up straight. He stayed motionless for a moment, then he was out of bed and heading to the front door. I grabbed my clothes and struggled into them as quickly as I could, not even stopping to do up the laces on my shoes in case I lost him.

By the time I managed to get outside, he was already at the other side of the parking lot, and I ran to try and catch up with him. He was naked and moving with more agility and speed than any sleeping person should have been able to, and it was difficult keeping up with him, but I managed to keep him in sight, even as he weaved his way through the trees.

All of a sudden, he stopped, and I slowed my approach, not wanting to startle him. At first, I thought it was the shadows from the moonlight through the trees, but as I got closer, I could see his torso rippling and contorting. Then he raised his head to the sky and howled, and he turned and looked directly at me.

My first instinct was to run, to get as far away from him as possible, but as I picked up pace and the branches grazed against my skin, I realized it wasn't fear I was feeling, it was exhilaration. My heart was pounding and my skin felt electrified. Everything was so clear; I could see every leaf on the trees, I could hear small creatures scurrying around in the undergrowth, and I could smell Rob on the breeze as he stalked me. My juices were already running down my thighs, and without thinking, I pulled off my top and pants.

I didn't know what he was, but I didn't care. I wanted him to take me, out here in the woods, like an animal. His scent was stronger, and a rush of heat against my shoulder caused me to moan. I didn't wait for him to grab hold of me, instead, I dropped to my hands and knees in the dirt and presented myself for his taking.

He entered me from behind, ramming his rock-hard cock into me as I fought to stay in position. I could feel the hair on his thighs as the slammed against the back of my legs, and his claws scraped at my back and hips, leaving searing hot welts in their wake. My inner muscles contracted sharply around his cock, and I panted and cried as I came. It spurred him on, and he grabbed both my hips and pounded into me as hard and as fast as he could until he suddenly stopped, and I could feel his hot seed filling me up. He howled when he came, and after a few grunts and growls, he withdrew and took off running into the darkness.

Everything hurt. My hands and knees from being pushed against the ground, my back where he'd scratched me, and my pussy from the ferocious fucking. I stayed as I was for a while, catching my breath and trying to make sense of what had happened, but how could I? Finally, I picked myself up, put my clothes back on, and slowly made my way back to the apartment. If Rob had really been coming out here all week rather than it being a dream, he'd be back in the morning, and we could try and figure out what the hell was happening together, but for tonight, all I wanted was a hot shower, and warm bed, and to sleep.

WHILE I WAS SLEEPING

WHILE I WAS SLEEPING

I lie in bed, waiting for the footsteps on the stairs.

During a conversation last week, James confessed that when he crawls into bed after working a late shift and I'm asleep, he feels this overwhelming urge to touch me, but he never does because he wouldn't know if I want him to or not.

He's great like that. He understands that sex is more than just a physical encounter, and if I'm not into it then neither is he. The guy I was with before James used to pressure me, and quite often I'd lie there and allow him to fuck me just to get it over with. But with James, the sex is always amazing because it's always wanted. Consent for us is not something to be assumed, but an integral part of foreplay and a way for us to voice exactly what we want from each encounter.

The idea of him wanting me when I'm asleep is exciting, but I understand his reservations, and I have some as well. What if I wasn't in the mood and woke up to find him trying to fuck me? Would that change the way I feel about him? But now he's mentioned it, I desperately want him to.

"What if…" I said, wrapping my arms around his waist and moving my mouth close to his ear, "I text you when I'm in the mood at bedtime. That way you'll know I want you, and you can do whatever you want to me when you get home."

Of course, he'd agreed, and today is his first late shift, so I shot off a text around ten pm, then waited for him to get home around midnight.

I know I'm supposed to be asleep, but I was already aroused just at the thought of him doing what he wanted to me, so I decided, this time at least, I would fake it. I put on a button-down nightshirt as I usually did, and settled myself under the covers with my e-reader. Then I dimmed the bedroom light and waited.

I'd chosen a steamy romance to help keep me in the mood, not that I needed much help, and as the heroine was swept of her feet by the handsome and muscular CEO, I couldn't help but slip my hand between my legs and gently rub my clit. As the CEO threw the heroine on the bed and stood over her with his large cock in his hand, I envisioned it was James standing over me as I slept. And when the CEO rammed his cock deep inside the heroine and fucked her into oblivion, I wondered if he would be more or less enthusiastic if she were asleep.

The silence was broken by the low rumble of a car engine getting closer, and I put the e-reader to one side and listened. It grew closer, then stopped outside the house, and I heard the sound of a car door shutting followed by footsteps and a key in the front door lock.

As soon as I heard him on the stairs, I closed my eyes and willed my body to relax. James entered the bedroom quietly, and I listened to him undress while I worked on keeping my breathing even. He sat on the side of the bed for what seemed like forever, and I knew he was watching me even if I couldn't see him.

Then he reached out and gently moved a strand of hair from my face. I stayed still and his hand moved down my shoulder and brushed against my breast. He paused for a moment, then pulled the sheets down to reveal the rest of me. Again his hand, gentle, on my thigh this time, moved upward to my hip. Then he fumbled with the buttons on my nightshirt, trying not to wake me as he popped each one open.

I was already sensitive to every movement he made, and when he pulled my nightshirt open, the feel of the fabric brushing my skin sent ripples of pleasure through my body. James ran a single finger around my breasts, first the left, then the right, before taking one of my nipples between his finger and thumb. I heard his sharp intake of breath as my nipple hardened, and he squeezed slightly as he lowered his head to my other breast. His breath was hot against my skin and I fought the urge to raise my chest up to meet his mouth. Then his tongue was circling my other nipple, flicking against it, sending shockwaves all the way to my clit.

I shifted my head on the pillow, and he stopped, waiting to see if he'd woken me up. Part of me wanted to open my eyes and kiss him, to throw the whole scenario out of the window and just lose myself in him, but this was too intense to stop. He moved his mouth back to my breast, then kissed down my stomach. His lips were like fire against my skin, and not being able to see or move was sending my senses into overdrive. His hand slid over my thigh, reaching between my legs, and I shifted my position to open my legs slightly. He took the opportunity to pull at my thigh, opening my legs even more, and then his mouth was on my mound.

His tongue lapped at my opening and he groaned against my skin, sending the heat of his breath deep inside me. I knew I was wet because his mouth slipped over my pussy lips with ease while his tongue found my clit. He sucked it into his mouth and I couldn't stop my body from bucking against him, but his focus was concentrated between my legs and he didn't stop to see if he'd woken me. My entire body was on fire, and my internal muscles were spasming as I headed towards the most intense orgasm I'd ever had.

All my focus was on my clit and the way his tongue was swirling around it. I tried as hard as I could to breath, but even with my eyes closed I could see stars appearing in front of me. I relaxed all my muscles as best I could, and when he sucked at my clit again I let the feeling rage through me as I orgasmed against his mouth.

The stars expanded into fireworks, and the heat in my body became an inferno as I bucked and writhed against him. His mouth disappeared and he shifted on the bed until he was between my legs. He lifted my knees to position himself and I could feel the hardness of his cock pushing against my opening. Then he pushed his hands between my ass and the bed and lifted me into the perfect position.

He entered me while I was still reeling from the last orgasm, and I could feel every millimetre of him pushing inside me. He was harder and bigger than I'd ever felt and he thrusted with the power of desperate need. He was past caring if I was asleep or awake any more, I could feel it in his movements, but I kept up the pretence and lay there, unresponsive to his assault, and just felt his movements inside me.

My lips stretched around him, and my internal muscles clasped against him, holding him in place as he moved inside me, and the rhythmical pounding against my clit as he filled me over and over to the hilt was incredible. Every single minuscule movement was magnified and I slipped into oblivion as he slid against my g-spot. My second orgasm was every bit as powerful as the first, but it started deep within me, radiating out like a flower until no part of my body was left unaffected. Where stars appeared the first time, there was now an entire universe, and I felt disconnected yet connected to every atom of my being.

He thrusted harder as my muscles contracted harshly around him, then he pushed himself as deep into me as possible and came inside me with a muffled cry. His cock was pulsating, spilling his seed into me, and his arms stiffened around my sides for a moment before he lay his head on my stomach and sobbed against my skin.

The spasming of my muscles subsided along with his erection, and he eased himself from inside me, leaving me feeling like a part of me had disappeared. He eased himself up the bed and pressed against my side, laying kisses on my arm, shoulder and neck. Then he pulled the sheets up and wrapped his arms around me, and a few minutes later he was snoring softly against my neck.

I lay there awake for a while, breathing in his scent and basking in the heat from his skin. My body was still trembling from my multiple orgasms, and my pussy throbbed gently as a reminder of the pounding it had just taken. A smile spread across my face as I thought about what had just happened. James could have done anything he wanted to me, I'd given him permission to, but even when he could have been as selfish as he wanted to be, he'd still concentrated on satisfying me first, and if that wasn't true love, then it doesn't exist.

James never knew I was awake. I let him recount the night to me over coffee the following morning, and he spent a good while marvelling about how my body responded to his touch even when I was asleep, and how he had made me come twice. He asked if maybe I'd dreamed about it while my body was reacting to his, and I told him I didn't remember, but I'd woken up feeling happy and satisfied. Then he asked if I regretted it as I wasn't awake to participate, and I laughed. Far from regret, I couldn't wait until his next late shift so I could play the fantasy out for real, but until then, I was more determined than ever to show him just how much I loved him, and just how skilled I could be with my lips and tongue.

REVENGE IS SWEET

CHAPTER ONE

"You're still not speaking to me? Really?" Mom stood outside my bedroom door, and the wood creaked as she leant against it. "Seriously, Mel, you can't keep being mad at me for what happened. You know I was drunk, and it wasn't as if he was your boyfriend or anything."

I held my breath, waiting for her to finish talking and go away.

"Look, I don't have time for this now. I'm going to miss my flight. We'll talk when I get back, okay?"

She shuffled her feet, but I refused to answer her.

"I'll text you when I get there. Oh, and Mike is coming over at two to pick up the dogs, so make sure you're here to let him in."

I sat up in bed, listening for the door shutting, and once I was sure she'd left, I jumped out of bed and headed for the shower, determined to show her two can play at that game.

Cade may not have been my boyfriend, but he was my friend, and walking in on him with his cock buried deep inside my mother was not something I ever want to see again. And she couldn't see that she'd done anything wrong. He was nineteen, for fuck sake, and she was in her forties, and it was disgusting. Besides, he was mine, or should have been, and probably would have been if we'd spent a bit more time together, but how could I think about him like that after seeing what I did, and she had taken him away from me.

The shower spat a few times before raining warm water down on my head, and I grabbed my razor, starting on my legs. Could I do this? Even after fucking Cade, Mom still held out hope that her and Mike would get back together. He'd lived with us for ten years before their relationship fizzled out, I'd even called him Dad, and after a year separation, she was laying the groundwork to get him back by having him dog-sit. Well, fuck you, Mom. If you can screw someone of mine, I'm sure as shit going to try and screw someone of yours.

With my legs smooth, I shaved my underarms, and then I turned my attention to my pussy. I'd read online that having a clean-shaven pussy was a huge turn-on for some men, and I needed all the ammunition I could get to convince Mike to fuck me.

It would be easy for me, as truth be told I'd harbored a bit of a crush on him ever since Mom introduced me to him, but I was only ten at the time and I knew he would never think about me the way I thought about him, so I pushed it deep inside. But that was a long time ago, and maybe as I'd grown up he'd considered me as something more than a young girl he'd parented. It would make things simpler if he had, and the thought of him fantasizing about me send a sharp pang of delight through my body.

I turned the shower off, ran a towel over my body, and headed for my bedroom. It was around noon, and I had two hours to spare, so I grabbed my vibrator from my bedside table, closed my eyes, and imagined Mike lying next to me.

His hands ran over my breasts, circling around my nipples, and he leant over and took each one into his mouth in turn. I used one hand to mimic his mouth and lips while my other hand held the vibrator against my pussy and clicked the button.

The sudden tremor flowed through my clit and my body bucked in response. I licked my lips and increased the setting, lowering my other hand to my opening. I was wet and sensitive, and as the vibrator stimulated my clit, I pushed two fingers inside me.

I visualized Mike on top of me, his hard cock thrusting in and out of my pussy as I finger-fucked myself toward orgasm. Pressure built behind my clit, fanning outward to every part of my body, and just when I thought I couldn't take any more, my body released the pressure in a wave of muscle contractions.

My hand was soaked with my juices as my inner muscles gripped my fingers, and my head became fuzzy with delicious delight. I pulled the vibrator away and let my body work its way through my orgasm naturally, and when my muscles finally stopped spasming, I felt a tingling warmth through every part of me.

I lay there for a while, basking in my afterglow, and imagining Mike holding me close in his big, strong arms. Would he be this attentive in real life? And what would his cock look and feel like? Suddenly, getting back at Mom didn't seem so important, as I realized my plan to try and fuck Mike was just as much a response to my own pent-up sexual frustration as any need for revenge.

It was a little after one now, and I had less than an hour until Mike was due to arrive, so I forced myself up from the bed, cleaned my vibrator, and started rummaging through my drawers and wardrobe for something to wear.

Everything I tried seemed too mundane or formal, and in the end, I opted for a cheeky tshirt with an image of an open mouth and a banana, and nothing else. The shirt was long enough to cover my ass, but short enough for me to accidentally display myself to him if I bent over without any underwear on.

A quiet giggle escaped my mouth as I tested my outfit in the full-length mirror, and I pulled my hair into a high pigtail and smeared the slightest bit of pink gloss on my lips. I looked both sexy and innocent at the same time, and I practiced my coy smile a few times before setting my phone to record in the corner of the room and skipping downstairs to wait.

He was exactly on time, as he always was, and he rang the

doorbell three times, as he always did. I counted to fifty before answering so he didn't know I'd been waiting for him, and I threw the door open and greeted him with a big smile. Mike gave me a lopsided grin in return and threw his arms around me.

"Hey, Mel, how are you doing?" He pulled back and gave me a kiss on the cheek before heading into the house to look for the dogs.

"I'm good, Mike. It's great to see you." I followed behind him as he made his way to the kitchen, my heart pounding with excitement.

"Mike? What happened to Daddy? Or are you too old for that now?"

"Sorry, Daddy," I said with a giggle. "Maybe I am too old, I don't know."

"Don't worry, sweetheart. You may be all grown up now, but you'll always be my little girl. And there they are, come here babies!"

Milo and Pepper ran toward him with their tails wagging at full speed, and he went down on his knees to fuss them.

"Do you have time for a coffee?" I said, moving into a position where he would see my naked pussy if he looked up, but he kept his focus on the dogs.

"Of course. I've always got time to hang out with you."

I walked to the other side of the kitchen and reached up to get the coffee from the cupboard, and it hadn't crossed my mind that my tshirt would lift as I raised my arms until Mike coughed. I pretended not to hear it and carried on filling the coffee machine, chatting about how my receptionist job was going and how I was considering a move to sales, all the time trying to keep myself calm and focused so not to scare him off.

When the coffee machine started spluttering, I turned around to find him standing up and fiddling with a pile of junk mail in order to avoid looking at me. He'd definitely seen that I wasn't wearing any panties, as his erection was straining against his jeans, and while he seemed to be embarrassed, he hadn't told me to get dressed or left. Maybe he didn't want to make me feel awkward, or maybe…

I decided to go with the second maybe, and I sat on top of the oak kitchen table and placed a foot on one of the chairs. My legs were slightly open, and my raised knee gave him a perfect view between my thighs. I could feel my wetness on my skin, and my pussy throbbed gently at the thought of being exposed while my cheeks reddened at the thought of being rejected.

I watched him as he busied himself, how his thick, dark hair gave him a boyish look, and how his muscles moved beneath his tshirt, and I wanted him to touch me so much.

He glanced over at me, and his eyes dropped to my pussy. I widened my legs, making it clear that this wasn't a mistake, that I wanted him to see me, and he coughed again, turning his head away from me.

"Mel, I'm not comfortable with this."

It wasn't what I wanted to hear, but I was all-in at this point, so I countered him.

"Neither am I, Daddy. In fact, I'm really uncomfortable right now, and the only thing that will make me feel better is for you to fuck me." I lowered a hand and pushed a finger inside my opening. "Don't tell me you've never thought about it. I have, but you were with Mom so I kept it to myself. Now you're not, so if you've ever wanted to fuck my tight little pussy, now's your chance."

I couldn't see his face, but the skin on his neck was turning a delicious scarlet color, so I continued.

"I bet everything I own that you've wondered what I taste like, or how my mouth would feel around your gorgeous cock. I know I've wondered what it would be like to suck your cock, and if I'd even be able to fit it in my mouth."

"Where is this coming from, Mel?" He shuffled awkwardly toward the sink, poured himself a glass of water, and took a gulp. "Do you even know what you're doing?"

Did I know what I was doing? There was no doubt in my mind that I did. I was getting revenge on Mom, but I also desperately wanted him to kiss me, to fuck me, to use my body, to make me come. I was doing whatever it took to get the satisfaction I craved, and he was the man I'd chosen to give it to me.

CHAPTER THREE

I slipped from the table, removed my tshirt, and walked over to him. "I know exactly what I'm doing. I'm giving myself to you because I want you to know every inch of me."

I took hold of his hand and brushed it against my firm breasts. He still wouldn't look at me, but he didn't fight what I was doing, so I lowered it to my pussy and let him feel how smooth my skin was down there and how wet I was for him.

The sound of his breath being sucked in past his teeth let me know that he wanted this as much as I did, even if he was holding back, and I lifted his hand to his face for him to smell my arousal.

He stood still for a moment, his breathing heavy as he took in my scent, and then he placed his fingers in his mouth and sucked my juices from them. I reached down and rubbed his hard cock through his jeans, and he groaned, turned around, and grabbed the back of my head, pulling me in for a kiss.

God, he tasted good. His hot breath filled my lungs as his

tongue swirled around mine, and a mixture of mint, coffee, and my own juices set my taste-buds alight.

He didn't stop kissing me until he'd back me into the table and lifted me up to sit on the edge with my legs wrapped around his waist, and then he lowered his head, running kisses down my neck, shoulders, and all the way to my breasts.

I couldn't help but moan as his warm tongue circled around my nipples, turning them into hard little balls of pleasure, and I cried out softly when he took each of them in turn between his teeth and sucked them into his mouth.

He raised his head and smiled at me, and then he pushed me back against the cool wooden surface and began kissing his way down my stomach.

"I need to taste you so badly right now." His words were interspersed with his lips against my skin, and as he brushed against the smoothness of my mound he whispered, "Oh, fucking Jesus," before grabbing my thighs, pushing my legs wide apart, and spreading my folds with his thumbs.

The first touch of his tongue against my clit caused my body to buck against him, and my entire body bristled with need. He paused briefly, holding me in place, and then he lapped around my opening and pushed his tongue as deep inside me as he could, swallowing my juices, before turning his focus back to my clit.

My hands waved around, desperate for something to grab hold of, but there wasn't anything, so I reached down and knotted my fingers into his hair.

"Hhmmm, I've only just started, and you can't control yourself." He pulled his face away from my pussy and moved my hands from his hair. "I've a feeling I'd end up without any hair if I let you carry on, so let's get you more comfortable first."

He pulled me back into a sitting position and rummaged through one of the kitchen drawers until he found a roll of food wrap. I couldn't work out what he was doing until he placed my arms, hands to elbows, behind my back and used the wrap to bind them together before laying me back down.

My arms were held tightly beneath me, with no room to move them. This was the first time I'd been restrained in any way, and it was exciting and scary at the same time, and when he lowered his head back down to my pussy, I realized just why people enjoyed restraints so much.

Without the ability to move my upper body, all my focus was shifted to my pussy, and the way my back was arched stretched my muscles and enhanced every touch.

He spread my pussy lips wide and began circling and flicking his tongue against my clit. Sparks shot through me, reaching deep into my stomach and sending my muscles into a string of mini-spasms, and I tried to move but I couldn't.

Pressure built behind my clit as he licked and sucked, expanding outward until it felt as if my whole body was about to explode, and then I was screaming and panting as my orgasm tore through me, every muscle contracting and releasing to the rhythm of his tongue.

I begged between breaths for him to stop this heavenly torture, but he pushed two fingers inside me, fucking me while my inner muscles clamped down against them. My skin was on fire, and my mind began to float as a second orgasm began to build before the first had fully subsided.

I gasped for air as stars and fireworks filled my vision, my body convulsed and twisted, and I couldn't even comprehend the idea of words let alone speak them. I was so far gone that I didn't even notice him slipping his fingers out from inside me, or his tongue no longer moving against my clit, and I barely registered him lifting me up and freeing my arms and holding me tight against him.

"Mel, are you okay?"

I tried to answer, but everything was muddled, and sounds tingled and tickled in my throat causing me to giggle. I rested my ear to his chest, listening to his heartbeat as I laughed, letting it calm me until I could focus again.

"Wow, that was… I've never…"

"I think you enjoyed it." He moved back and lifted my head, and he kissed me gently on the lips. "Do you still want me to fuck you, or do you want me to leave?"

"Leave? We've only just got started, haven't we?" I kissed him back as I moved my legs, testing to see if they would hold my weight. "You know what I taste like now, but I don't know what you taste like. How about we go upstairs so I can find out?"

He didn't need asking twice, and he held my hand as I put my full weight on my legs, just in case I needed support. As soon as I knew I could safely carry my own weight, I led him to the hallway and up the stairs to my bedroom.

I couldn't wait to have his straining cock in my mouth, to pleasure him the way he'd just pleasured me, and I grappled with his belt buckle, trying and failing to open it. He laughed and took over, and had his belt and buttons undone and his jeans around his ankles in one quick move. I grabbed the bottom of his shirt and lifted it up, and he bent down to let me pull it over his head.

His chest was smooth and tanned, and his abs rippled beneath his skin. I'd never noticed just how toned and fit he was, and I ran my hands over his torso, feeling every inch of it, before hooking my fingers into his boxers and freeing his cock.

It was everything I hoped it would be. His cock stood to attention in front of me, framed by dark curly hair, and I licked my lips at the thought of tasting it. He was long and thick, and dark purple veins snaked around from the base to his circumcised tip.

I dropped to my knees in front of him and wrapped my fist

around it. His hand stroked my hair as I gave him a cheeky grin and a wink before licking a drop of pre-cum from his helmet and opening my mouth as wide as I could.

I could barely take him in my mouth, so I used my tongue to flick across his tip while I squeezed gently with my hand and moved it up and down his length. My other hand reached for his balls, playing across them and massaging the skin behind them, and Mike groaned and grabbed a handful of my hair, pulling my head forward.

I tried to relax my jaw muscles, and I sucked and licked as he thrust himself in and out of my mouth, taking him in deeper with every movement. He tasted salty and musky as he moved against my tongue, and I quickened my pace, wanting to fully taste him. He responded by thrusting harder, and I opened up my throat as much as I could to take him. It was getting hard to breath, with less time to grab air between thrusts, but I knew he was close to coming as his balls were tightening in my grip.

Both his hands wrapped themselves in my hair, and he held me securely as he pounded against my face. I clawed at his stomach as panic started to set it from a lack of oxygen, and that was all he needed to take him over the edge. He thrust as deep as he could and gripped me tightly as he squirted cum into my mouth and throat, his cock pulsing against my tongue, and I swallowed as quickly as possible, but there was too much, and it seeped out from the sides of my mouth.

Finally, he was done, and he loosened his grip on my head. I pulled away and took a deep breath, followed by another, and then I grinned up at him.

"Did I do okay?" I used a finger to wipe the dribbles of cum from my lips and chin, and I sucked it suggestively as I held his gaze.

"Oh, sweet girl, you have no idea how skilled you are." He flopped back on the bed and sighed. "But I'm not as young as I used to be, so it may take me a while to get up and running again."

"That's okay." I straddled his waist and ran my hands gently across his chest. "We've got plenty of time."

"Play with your breasts." He placed his arms behind his head and stared at me with a half-smile playing across his face.

I ran my hands slowly up my stomach and circled them around my breasts before cupping and lifting them. They filled my hands, and I pushed them together to create a cleavage, before raising each one and bowing my head to lick my own nipples.

I could feel his cock twitching and rising beneath me, and I threw my head back and moaned loudly as I took my nipples between my fingers and thumbs and rolled them around. The feeling was delicious, but it was knowing the effect it was having on Mike that was the real turn-on.

CHAPTER FIVE

So much for him being too old to get another erection so soon. His cock was already hard, and it poked at me, eager to find my opening. I lifted myself up and used my hand to position him perfectly before lowering slowly onto him.

Even though he was huge, my wetness helped him slide in easily. My pussy lips were stretched to breaking point, and I felt so overwhelmingly full, I dared not move for fear of bursting. It took him moving his hip upward for me to begin riding him, and even then, I controlled his thrusts until I got used to the pounding my body was taking.

The slow movements may have helped Mike control himself, but every thrust rubbed against my g-spot, and an exquisite feeling of tightening pressure began to build inside me. It was different to anything I'd experienced before, and although I recognized it as the beginnings of an orgasm, it was far deeper and entwined with every part of me than any other orgasm I'd had.

I rode him faster, taking him deeper with every thrust, and I reveled in the heat that was spreading through my core. My muscles thrummed and sparked, my nerves ignited, and when I came, I fell apart around him, becoming fragments of myself spinning and dancing to the beat of my climax.

I fell forward, wanting to bask in my post-orgasmic bliss, but Mike was nowhere near finished, and he had other ideas. He tipped me sideways onto the bed, rolled me onto my stomach, and pulled my waist up to meet his hips.

He rammed his cock as far as it would go into my pussy, and I mewled at the sudden onslaught. It was painfully sweet as he impaled me over and over, and he grabbed my hair and pulled my head back while he took my doggy style.

I barely had any energy left, so when he withdrew and positioned himself against my puckered asshole, I had no other choice but to relax and take him. It wasn't the first time I'd been fucked in the ass, but he was bigger than I was used to, and my skin seared and burned as it tried to accommodate him.

"Please… Slow…" I panted through the words out through gritted teeth.

"Please, slow, what?" He paused his movements for a moment, waiting for my response. I didn't know what he meant or how to answer so I just repeated myself.

"Mike, please… go slow."

"Mike? Is that what you call me?" He rammed himself into my ass in what felt like a punishment.

"Sorry… Daddy… Please…."

His hand slid around my waist and made its way down to my clit, and his fingers pinched and squeezed, sending shock-waves through my pussy as his cock thrust in and out of my ass.

"Say my name again, you slutty little girl."

I had no idea how we got to this, but the next thing I knew, I was screaming words out, egging him on.

"Fuck me, Daddy. Fuck your little slut of a girl. Make me come around your massive cock."

Between his cock in my ass, his fingers on my clit, and the effect the words I was screaming were having on me, it wasn't long before I was bucking against him and my inner muscles were gripping his cock. I felt him grow even bigger and harder, and he roared as he came. His cock pulsed, and I could feel the heat of his seed squirting inside me, and my pussy muscles clenched around him, milking him for every last drop of cum he had.

He stayed inside me for a few minutes more until his cock began to soften, and then he slid out slowly and kissed down the length of my spine. We both collapsed on the bed, sweat-covered and breathless, and we lay there in silence trying to comprehend what had happened. Eventually, Mike spoke.

"This is pretty fucked up, Mel, don't you think?"

Now the excitement of reeling him in had faded and I thought about what we'd done, he was sort of right. There are lines we're not supposed to cross, and this was a pretty big fucking line. But even so…

"Yeah. But it was kinda fun." I tilted my head and gave him a cheeky grin.

"It was more than fun. You were amazing. But I feel as if I've violated you, and I should never have acted the way I did." He sat up on the bed and reached for his clothes, and he was back to not making eye contact with me. "I don't want things to change between us, Mel. I love you, always, but I think it would be a good idea if we took some time to figure out what happened here."

"And there was me thinking this was the start of some mind-blowing romance." I spotted the panic in his face straight away and stopped joking around. "I'm kidding. Jeez, take it easy."

"Maybe we can joke about this one day, I hope we can, but… Look, I really need to go."

I wrapped myself up in the bedsheets and watched as he finished dressing and practically ran down the stairs.

He spent another five minutes or so getting the dogs into their harnesses and collecting their food and bedding, and I could hear their whiny yaps as he walked them into the hallway.

"I'm off now," he shouted up the stairs. "Take care of yourself, Mel." The front door slammed, and ten seconds later his car door opened and closed.

Once I was sure I was alone again, I headed back to the shower. My body was tingling and aching, and my asshole burned and throbbed. That had been the most intense sexual experience I'd had, and regardless of whether it was right or wrong, I didn't regret a minute of it.

Of course, it would have been a better ending if Mike had at least wanted it to happen again, but he didn't, and there wasn't anything I could do to change that, and it did make what I was about to do a bit easier.

Once I'd washed away the dried cum from my ass and thighs, I slipped into a dressing gown and retrieved my phone from the bedroom shelf. I'd forgotten it was there the whole time we were fucking, and I giggled as I played back bits of the recording.

Most of the time all that could be seen was a mass of limbs, or my ass moving up and down as I rode him to ecstasy, and I felt a pang of regret that I wouldn't get to do this again with him. I shoved that feeling to one side, reminding myself that there were other men and other experiences, and maybe one or more of them would prove to be even better at fucking than Mike, and I focused on the video. There it was, the perfect shot.

Both our faces were in full view as Mike ground himself in and out of my ass doggy style. I had my mouth open, gasping for breath and moaning loudly, and my head was being pulled back by Mike's fist in my hair. He had his eyes closed, and his expression was one of intense concentration as he rammed into me.

I paused the video and took a screenshot, and then I stopped for a moment. There would be no take-backs. If I continued, I'd be destroying any future relationship I could possibly have with Mike, but then I remembered walking in on Mom and Cade, and how she turned her head to the side and made eye contact with me, smiling as he pumped away on top of her. I remembered shaking my head and bursting into tears before running to my room, and how instead of realizing what she was doing was wrong, she ignored my tears and carried on fucking him for another hour at least.

And I remembered how she belittled me afterward, reminding me that he wasn't mine, and it was only sex so there was nothing to be upset about, and she was sorry I'd walking in on them, but I should be more mindful of her privacy.

Mindful!

I opened the text messages on my phone, attached the screenshot from the video, and began typing.

> *HI MOM.*
> *JUST SO YOU KNOW, IT WAS ONLY SEX.*
> *AND IT'S OK BECAUSE HE'S NOT YOURS*
>   *ANYWAY.*
> *LOVE YOU.*
> *MEL.*

CHEATING DEATH

CHAPTER ONE

Jeanette leaned forward on the barstool and motioned towards the bartender. He smiled and nodded as he held a glass under the tap for the customer at the other side of the bar.

"Same again?" he said, and she mouthed 'please', waiting for him to turn back to his bar duties before subtly undoing a button on her blouse to reveal more of her cleavage.

Nerves made her stomach clench and unclench, and she did her best to hide them as he grabbed the bottle of white wine and poured her another glass.

As he turned and slid the glass in front of her, his eyes came to rest on the enhanced shape of her breasts, and he leaned forward. He smelled of spilled whiskey, sliced limes, and cheap deodorant, which wasn't her ideal mixture, but at least it was bearable.

"Are they to your liking?" she said with a smile, waiting to see how he reacted.

"They're impressive," he responded, lifting his eyes to her and holding her attention.

It was the sign she was looking for as she didn't have the time for game playing.

"Do you want to see the rest of me?"

He rubbed his hand on his chin and tilted his head.

"Are you suggesting a date?"

"I wouldn't put it that way." She ran her fingers down the middle of her cleavage and carried on the movement all the way to her pussy. His eyes followed. "I'm not interested in getting to know you over dinner. I want to fuck you, preferably tonight."

She opened her legs slightly and slipped her hand between them, wanting to hold his full attention.

"I finish in thirty, but I can probably get off sooner," he said.

"The sooner the better," she replied. "I'm just going to find the bathroom to freshen up."

"One thing before you go," he said, as she slipped off the stool. "You didn't tell me your name."

Jeanette glanced back at him over her shoulder and smirked. "I know."

She didn't know what she expected, but the bathroom was pristine. Most bars she'd been to had peeling paintwork, stains that you really didn't want to think what they were on the doors and floors, and faucets that dribbled if you were lucky, but they were usually the types of places that were slammed on the weekends whereas this was a quieter establishment.

She unhooked her bag from her shoulder, placed it on the countertop, and fished around until she found the photograph she was looking for. The man in the picture could have been the twin of the guy behind the bar, if it weren't for the different eye and hair color.

"Hi, baby," she said, staring at the image. "You won't believe this, but I think I've found the right guy." She placed the photograph next to her and ran a brush through her hair. "He'll need a bit of work. I've already got the colored contact lenses, and I can grab some hair dye next week."

She reached back in her bag, picked up a tube of mascara, and applied it to her eyelashes. "I think he's really into me as well, which is going to make the evening go so much smoother, don't you think?" She checked her teeth and practiced her smile, before picking up the photograph and running her thumb across it. "We're almost there. Hold, on, baby."

After placing her lips against the image, she placed it back in her bag and opened the bathroom door.

CHAPTER TWO

The house was a large, wooden structure at the end of a long driveway. Jeanette had been lucky enough to get a good deal on it after the last owners declared bankruptcy, and it afforded her not only the space she needed but a level of privacy most people only dream of.

The bartender made himself at home straight away, taking his jacket off and throwing it on the sofa before following her into the kitchen and pushing her up against the table. His arms wrapped around her and he nuzzled his nose against her ear.

"So, what do you want me to do to you?" he said, and he reached for the buttons on her blouse. She pushed him away and moved to the other side of the kitchen and pulled a bottle of whiskey from a cupboard.

"oh no, baby, tonight isn't about me. Why don't you head on through to the bedroom and get yourself comfortable, and I'll bring the drinks through? It's the hallway the other side of the living room, third door on the left."

Jeanette kept an eye on him as he sauntered through the living room towards the bedroom, and once he was out of sight she filled a glass with the whiskey. She closed her eyes and placed her hand over the top of the glass, and whispered something against her fingers, and then she raised the glass and took a sniff of the contents. A smile broke out on her face, and she swirled the liquid around and carried it to the bedroom.

He was splayed out on the bed waiting for her. His muscles were firm, and his skin was lightly tanned and blemish free, and his large cock was already erect. The sight of him was mesmerizing, and she stopped for a moment and silently thanked her lucky stars for finding someone so perfect.

"Here's your drink," she said and held the glass out to him, and once he'd taken it from her hand, she sauntered over to the stereo in the corner. A sultry rhythm and blues song burst into the air, and Jeanette closed her eyes and swayed to the music. She ran a hand across her stomach, then up and over her breasts as she moved. The bed creaked, and she know he was sitting up to watch her, so she undid the buttons on her blouse and let it fall to the floor before reaching around to unto the zip of her skirt.

She opened her eyes and looked at him. He'd barely touched his drink; his focus was on her and only her.

"Would you like me to take off my bra?" she said, and he nodded as he ran his hand up and down his straining cock. "Then drink up." He did as he was instructed, and once the glass was empty Jeanette unhooked her bra while holding it in place. She lowered it slowly, allowing the sheer lace to play against her nipples before letting it fall.

"Are these to your liking?"

He leaned forward. "Do you know how amazingly sexy you are?"

"And what exactly would you like to do to my amazingly sexy body?" She hooked a finger into her lace panties, slid them down her legs, and crawled onto the bed next to him.

"I want to suck those perfect nipples, and I want to bury my cock deep inside you and fuck you 'till you scream," he said, and reached out to grab her.

She pushed him down on the bed and ran a hand over his chest before lowering her mouth to his cock. He groaned and grabbed her hair to hold her in place, and she licked around his helmet before taking as much of him in her mouth as she could manage. He tried to say the words "oh, fuck," but he couldn't quite form them. His grip on her hair loosened, and he tried to push her away. "Some... something... no... wrong..."

"It's okay, baby. Just go with it," she said and resumed sucking his cock. His hand caught the side of her face, but he didn't have the strength to do any damage. She lifted her head and watched him as he scrambled around weakly trying to pull himself up off the bed. His skin was glistening with sweat, and his eyes were unfocussed.

"Just lie down and let it happen," she said, and she gently pushed him back against the sheets. She reached under a pillow and found the restraints she'd hidden, and then she tied his ankles and wrists to the posts of the bed, making sure he couldn't escape from them if he regained some strength.

O nce she was fully convinced he was secure, she made her way to the chest of drawers at the other side of the room and pulled out a large black marble bowl, incense, and a dozen pillar candles, and placed them carefully on the top of the dresser.

The man on the bed moaned, and Jeanette stopped what she was doing and took hold of his wrist, checking his pulse. It was slow, but it was steady, and she leaned down and spoke quietly into his ear until he relaxed again.

She was almost ready, but there was one thing missing. After wrapping a robe around her naked body, she made her way through the living room and kitchen and out to the back yard. The chicken coup was in wire enclosure, and she lifted the catch and let herself in as quietly as she could. The rooster stirred as she slipped the bag over its head and stilled again as she lifted it into her arms and carried it back to the bedroom.

With her free hand, she grabbed a box of matches and began

lighting the candles. "Papa Legba," she said, "ouvrier barrier pour moi agoe." She lit the incense and moved her hand above it to disperse the scent into the room. As she lit the rest of the candles, she repeated the words, the desperation in her heart causing her voice to shake. As soon as the final candle was lit, a sudden breeze brushed over her skin and the flames began to dance. She lowered her head in submission and welcomed his presence.

The rooster began to struggle as she removed it from the bag. It was a truly magnificent bird, powerful and strong, and she had to use all her strength to hold it. Its talons swiped at the air and its feathers scratched against her chest, but she continued her chant as she reached for a ceremonial knife and slid it smoothly into the rooster's neck.

Blood sprayed from the wound, coating her face and everything on the dresser as the bird flapped its wings wildly. Eventually it gave up fighting, and Jenette held it over the bowl, collecting the blood that was left.

The breeze picked up, and it seemed to dance around her, cooling the blood on her skin and sending chills through her body, but there wasn't time to worry about that. She picked up the bowl and carried it carefully to the bed. She dipped her fingers into the blood and began drawing intricate patterns onto the skin of the barman, and as she kept on chanting, they radiated light.

The breeze became heated, as she made her way back to the dresser, hot breath on her body that warmed and comforted. She dropped some twigs into the blood-filled bowl followed by ripped up pieces of paper, and then she broke up a cigar and crumbled the tobacco over the top. As soon as she lit it, a funnel of smoke lifted from the bowl and circled the room.

"You called me, chile?"

The voice was a deep rumble and it seeped into her ears and deep inside her.

"Papa Legba, I have an offering for you."

The smoke funnel moved to the middle of the room and lowered itself over the barman, covering his entire body in a haze.

"Do you know what you are doing, chile? This soul is not a willing sacrifice, and as such will sit as a heavy darkness on my heart. Your soul in exchange for this is welcome, but for such an exchange you will have to provide your light sooner than you may like." A tendril of smoke lifted from the man on the bed and coiled itself around her.

"It's worth the price, and when you call I will provide my light happily."

As soon as she spoke those words, the man on the bed gasped for breath. He pulled against the restraints, fighting against the inevitable, but with each movement he became weaker, and finally he exhaled and stilled.

The smoke lifted and wrapped itself around her, and she could feel it pulling at her soul, testing her resolve.

"Time is not your friend, chile," it whispered against her skin. "It is fleeting, and you will regret this choice." By the time it finished speaking, it was nothing more than a faint echo in the back of her mind.

Jeanette's legs gave way and she sank to the floor. Tears cascaded down her face as she thought about what she'd just promised. There was no way she'd just give up willingly to

Papa Legba when the time came, no matter what she had said, but what would that mean for her soul?

CHAPTER FOUR

She shook her head. There was no time to be afraid right now. She knew the body on the bed was starting to cool already, and she had to get herself moving. Her mind began to clear as she ran through what needed doing, and she scrambled up from the floor and got to work.

After running to the kitchen and filling up a bucket of water, she began cleaning the blood off the body, starting at the feet and working her way up to the head. The clock was ticking, and her heart was pounding in her chest as she worked. What if it didn't work? What if she's sold her soul for nothing?

Quit that way of thinking right now.

Jeanette opened the bedroom closet and took out the urn that contained her husband's ashes. "It's almost time, baby. Come back to me," she whispered as she unscrewed the lid.

A tablespoon of ashes mixed with water in a vial she had ready as she gave it a shake, then she rummaged through a drawer for a syringe. Her hand shook as she filled it with the liquid and have it a squeeze to get rid of any air.

"This has to work," she said to herself, and she placed the needle against the arm of the bartender. There was the slightest bit of resistance, and then it slid into the skin. She pulled the plunger back to make sure she'd hit the vein, and it filled with blood, so she pushed until all the contents were gone.

"Vini non, anmòrèz mwen, nou p'ap gen ansanm."

Jeanette climbed on top of the man and pressed down on his chest while repeating the words.

There was nothing.

She pressed down again, and again.

The body remained motionless.

Another compression, and another.

"Please! Come back to me!" she screamed as tears ran down her face. She thumped her hands down over and over and over.

And then his chest rose and fell.

She stopped, her hands raised above her head.

No movement.

She leaned down and rested her ear to his chest, desperate to hear even a single beat. And there it was, followed by another and another, and her heart felt like it was being squeezed from her body.

"Max?"

She pushed herself up the bed, grabbed the face of the corpse, and forced a breath into its mouth. "Come on, honey. You can do this. Breath!" She exhaled again and watched.

Time seemed to stop, but finally there was the sharp rasping of air being sucked in through the windpipe, and the body twitched beneath her.

"Oh my God, Max? Please say it's you?"

"Jeannie?" The voice was hardly more than a faint whisper. "Where am I?"

Max attempted to sit up, but he was still secured to the bed. His eyes darted around the room in confusion as Jeanette untied the ropes and rubbed each of his limbs until the blood flow came back. Then she eased him up a bit and placed a pillow behind his head.

"Don't try to move," she said, and she kissed his cheeks and lips. "I will tell you everything, but we have to take it slowly."

"Thirsty," he whispered.

Jeanette curled up on the bed next to Max, watching him as he slept. His body might be different now, but everything that made him Max was the same. The way he crooked his arm beneath his head and the hint of a smile on his face as he breathed deeply and evenly were all him. She wanted to burst into laughter, but she held it back, not wanting to wake him. He was back, by her side, and the world was once again the way it should be.

He began mumbling to himself, and his eyes flicked back and forth behind his lids. She placed a hand on his arm to comfort him, and his eyes opened.

"Hey," he said, and smiled at her.

"Hey yourself," she replied and kissed him.

His smile disappeared, replaced with a frown.

"What's happened, Jeannie? I was having a strange dream, and everything seems hazy. And what's with my voice?"

She paused for a moment, not sure how to explain everything to him, and then would her fingers through his before she spoke. "You were in an accident, Max."

"Accident? I don't remember anything."

"It was a drunk driver. You were on your way home from the gym and he hit you side on."

"That can't be right," he said, flexing his arms and legs. I feel fine, apart from not sounding like myself. Did I injure my throat?"

Jeanette looked at him, trying to keep the tears from spilling down her face, and she couldn't find the words. Max sat up and took both her hands in his.

"You need to tell me everything," he said.

"They had to tear the car apart to get to you, and by the time…" All those feeling from that day came flooding back, and she felt the unbearable pain as the nurse held her tightly, and she remembered the police officer's uniform, soaked through with blood, and the way the surgeon pushed the doors open and took a step toward her before shaking his head, and she remembered screaming and screaming. She took a deep breath and held it, desperately willing the grief to subside.

"Breath, Jeannie! Don't do this." He shook her shoulders and she exhaled, the tears finally flowing. "What is it? Have I been in a coma? Is that why I don't remember anything?"

"I'm so sorry, Max," she said, and she hugged him as tightly as she could. "You died."

He stared at her for a moment, saying nothing, and then he started laughing. "Really? You pick a time like this to try and prank me? Your comedic timing has never been great, but this?"

"It was two years ago. By the time the managed to get you out of the car, you'd lost too much blood. The doctors worked on you for hours, but…"

"Dead? I don't know what's happening with you right now, but look at me, I'm not dead." He lifted his arms to show her, but then he stared at his hands, turning them over and over.

Jeanette stood up and motioned for him to join her. She walked him to the closet and pulled the door open to reveal the full-length mirror.

"Just look," she said, and she pushed him in front of it. "I brought you back."

She watched his reaction in the mirror as he reached up and ran his hands over his face, pulling on his cheeks and turning his face from side to side. He lowered his hands to his chest and rested them over his heart, and his forehead furrowed.

"This isn't possible. How is this possible?"

"Does that really matter?" Jeanette said, resisting the urge to reach out and touch him.

"But this isn't my body." He twisted from side to side, his eyes never leaving his reflection.

"It is now. And you'll get used to it," she said, and she moved forward and wrapper her arms around his waist. "The only thing that really matters is that you're here with me, and I'm here with you." She kissed his back, and his arm, and then swiveled herself around and kissed his chest, and neck, and chin, and when her lips brushed against his, he kissed her back.

It had been two, long, heartbreaking years of dreaming that everything was normal and having Max sweep her up in his strong arms, of placing her lovingly on the bed, and of kissing every inch of her body before easing himself inside her, only to wake up each morning to find it was all a cruel trick.

Now he was here, with her, his hands grabbing at her breasts, his mouth devouring hers. His new body would take time to come to terms with, but his passion was something she could lose herself in forever.

Jeanette moaned as his hand reached between her legs and found her clit, and she opened her thighs as far as possible as his deft fingers began to play. His teeth grazed down her neck, and he took each of her nipples into his mouth in turn, sucking and nibbling on them.

His need seemed almost greater than hers as he moved his head between her legs and began to devour her pussy. His lips forced her folds apart, and his nose pushed against her clit as his tongue pushed inside her, lapping her juices as she bucked and writhed against him. He was thirsty, desperate, and determined, and she grabbed the bedsheets tightly as her muscles tightened, the deep, internal pressure building fast and ferocious. Jeanette screamed as her orgasm exploded within her, sending her core into a searing meltdown. Her internal muscles clamped down on his tongue, and he groaned against her pussy. Her body convulsed, her head was swimming, and she gasped for breath as she clawed at the bed.

The assault on her pussy eased and Max crawled up her body and thrust his tongue into her mouth. Her senses filled with her own taste and smell, and she grabbed handfuls of his hair as her own tongue explored this new mouth. She needed him inside her, for his hard cock to fill her completely.

"Fuck me, Max," she cried into his mouth between kisses, and she reached a hand down to guide him into her.

He grabbed hold of her hand and raised it above her head. Then he grabbed her other hand and held them both fast as he positioned himself at her entrance. She lifted her legs and wrapped them around his back, and as his cock found her opening, she pushed against it.

He moved with her, teasing her with his tip.

"Please, oh God, please!"

"Is this what you want?" he said, grinning at her, and he moved his hips to run his cock over her soaking wet folds.

"You know it is," she said, her breath ragged.

"Are you sure this is what you want?" he said, his eyes never leaving hers.

She started to speak, and he thrust himself inside her, hard and fast. The barman's cock was thicker and longer than she was used to, and she felt as if she'd be ripped apart, but as Max began to move more slowly, her body adjusted and a wave of pleasure washed over her.

She held his eye contact as he thrust inside her, not daring to close her eyes in case this was yet another dream, but the weight of his body on top of her and the friction of his cock against her g-spot was real, and tears slid down the side of her face as she stared at him.

Her body felt electrified, and each thrust of his cock was bringing her closer to another orgasm. Heat coursed through her stomach, radiating outward, and she groaned with each exhaled breath.

Max was close as well. His forehead scrunched up and he lowered his head to her shoulder, his breath hot and heavy against her skin. He thrusted harder and faster, and she lifted her hip to meet his rhythm. Her orgasm blossomed inside her, spreading throughout her body until every part of her pulsed and tingled. Her inner muscles clung to his cock and he grunted with pleasure and rammed into her as hard and quick as he could. Then he was roaring in her ear as he pumped his seed deep inside her.

They panted in unison as Max collapsed on top of her, their sweat-covered bodies sliding against each other. Her muscles were still spasming gently, and his cock twitched in response as it slowly began to soften. Jeanette shifted her position, trying to hold him inside her, but he slipped out and his seed oozed down her thighs, leaving a wet stain on the sheets beneath her. He rolled over, gasping for air, and she shivered as sweat cooled on her skin.

For the first time in two years, she felt alive, happy, content, and she closed her eyes to fully enjoy the afterglow.

'Time is fleeting, Chile'. She pushed the echo in her head away and reached out a hand to stroke Max's chest. 'You will regret this'. Max's heartbeat was strong and even as he lay next to her, and he slipped an arm beneath her shoulders, drawing her closer as he sighed with contentment.

Time may be fleeting, she thought, *but there is nothing to regret.* Her life had been over, but now she had Max back, and she was going to make the most of every waking moment with him.

THE THERAPIST

The waiting room was empty as I sat watching the clock on the wall. I hadn't been to see a therapist since I was a child, and I had no idea if I would even be able to talk to him, but my friend Marcy had told me he was good, and his unconventional techniques were just what I needed, and I was desperate for someone to help me.

Eventually, the door opened, and a young woman walked past me dabbing her eyes with a tissue.

"Miss Anderson?" the therapist said, and I nodded. It was too late to make a run for the door, so I took a deep breath and followed him into his office.

"I'm sorry my receptionist wasn't there to greet you. You're my last patient of the day and she finishes early on a Friday."

"That's fine," I said, standing by the door and twisting my scarf in my fingers. "If you're waiting to get off home I can always make another appointment."

"No, of course not," he replied, motioning for me to take a seat on the large sofa. He sat opposite me. "Now what can I help you with, Miss Anderson?"

"Please, it's Alice," I said, trying to hide my nervousness.

"Alice it is. And you can call me Robert. So… would you like to tell me what's on your mind?"

I closed my eyes for a moment and took a deep breath, trying to center myself, and when I opened my eyes, I kept them focused on the floor while I spoke.

"It's stupid really. I don't even know why I'm here. Well… I do… but…"

Robert sat back in his chair, picked up a clipboard, and scribbled something down.

I stopped talking as I stared at his hands. I shouldn't be here was all I could think.

"Don't mind this, Alice. I take notes during all my sessions, but they are for my eyes only. I keep paper copies so there's no chance of your details getting out if we're hacked, and I make sure to lock them away securely when I've finished with them. Is that okay with you?"

"I guess so," I said, still fidgeting with my scarf. "I'm just worried that…"

"That all your deepest, darkest secrets will find their way into the big wide world?" He placed the clipboard to one side and sat forward with his hands knotted together. "Everyone thinks their secrets are deeper and darker than everyone else's, and everyone is scared of therapy at first. But trust me, it won't be long before you are feeling better about yourself, more in control, and happier with your life." He opened a cupboard underneath the coffee table that sat between us and took out two glasses and a bottle of sparkling water. "If you want, we can spend this session just chatting, until you're relaxed enough to tell me why you're really here."

I watched as he poured the water between the glasses, and then I picked up the one in front of me and took a sip. Just chatting would be nice, but I wasn't exactly affluent, and I'd kick myself for spending money on chatting as soon as I left.

"I expose myself," I blurted out. There, the hardest part was done. Now he could tell me what a deviant I am and how I need to change. But he didn't. Instead he picked his clipboard back up and gave me a smile.

"Now we have our starting point. I want you to think back to the first time you exposed yourself and how it made you feel."

"Okay… umm… It was around six months ago, and it wasn't much really. I was getting ready for a night out, and I was in my underwear going through my wardrobe. I was unsure what I wanted to wear so I was holding dresses up against myself in front of the mirror when the bedroom light in the house opposite lit up." I took another sip of water to compose myself. "It was then I realized that I'd left the bedroom curtains open and anyone could have seen me."

"And did anyone see you?"

"I don't know. I don't think so. And the idea that someone could have seen me like that mortified me… but it also excited me."

"What did you do, in that moment I mean?"

I could feel my face burning and I didn't know if I should tell him everything.

"Don't be ashamed or embarrassed. I doubt there's anything you could tell me that I haven't heard before."

I swallowed hard and tried to figure out how to put it into words; being open sexually wasn't something I was used to, and I'd always changed the subject rather than have to talk about sex.

"I… well… I umm… masturbated." There, I'd said it.

"So, you were turned on to the point where you had to come?"

"Yes. That's wrong, isn't it? Dirty, I mean."

"No, it's not wrong, or dirty. Tell me how it felt. I assume you've masturbated many times. Was this time different?"

Oh God, this was not what I was expecting. I didn't want to talk about this, but that familiar feeling was starting to build inside me, and I could feel myself getting wet. It was like I felt when exposing myself, only this time it was with words, and all of a sudden, I couldn't stop myself blurting out every detail.

"I closed the curtains straight away, but I could feel all these eyes on me, waiting for me to give them a show, so I did. I laid on the bed and spread my legs as wide as I could, then I sucked on my fingers to get them wet and thrust them into my pussy. In my head, all these strangers were standing around me, watching everything I did, and I wanted them to enjoy it as much as I was.

"I finger-fucked myself for a while, but even though I was turned on, I couldn't get to that point, so I pulled out my vibrator. It's a rabbit. You know, with the vibrating ears so you can fuck yourself and play with your clit at the same time. It did the trick. I thrust it in and out of me, crying with pleasure every time those ears brushed against my clit, and I screamed when I came." I'd closed my eyes to relive that feeling as closely as possible, and I could feel that delicious pressure building between my legs as I talked. "I was so wet, the bedsheets underneath me had soaked through. Before I knew what I was doing I'd slipped my fingers inside me to collect my juices and I was sucking on them as hard as I could. I've never felt that level of need or pleasure before."

My body shuddered as a mild orgasm rippled through my muscles, and I opened my eyes to see if the therapist was staring at me. He wasn't. His focus was back on his clipboard and he was scribbling frantically. I didn't know whether to say something to him or to just let him finish, and I could feel the flush of embarrassment as my face turned red. Eventually he looked up and smiled.

"Stand up for me, Alice."

I did as I was told, even though it added to the feeling of self-consciousness that was seeping into my brain.

"Now undress."

"Sorry, what?" Surely I must have misheard him.

"Undress. You want to know if this is some deviance you have that we can fix? I'm giving you permission to expose yourself. Let's see if this is simply a short-lived fantasy that will disappear as soon as you're challenged on it, or a deep-seated need, shall we?"

Even though I felt uncomfortable standing in front of him, my body responded to his request. My skin felt hot and tingly under my clothes, and the thought of freeing myself from them was overwhelming, and my heart pounded hard against my chest as his eyes moved downward from my face.

CHAPTER THREE

I unwrapped the scarf from around my neck and let it fall to the floor as I began unbuttoning my blouse. My nipples were already straining against the silk fabric, desperate to be freed, and I pulled the fabric from my shoulders and reached around to unhook my bra. I couldn't help but sigh as the air brushed over my breasts, and I cupped them with my hands, running my thumbs over my erect nipples. My skin erupted in goosebumps, and I trailed my hand down my stomach before reaching to the side to undo the zip on my skirt. Then I hooked my fingers into my panties and slid them down.

The therapist's eyes never left my body as I undressed, and now I was standing naked before him he leaned forward and made eye contact again.

"How do you feel right now?"

"Hot, excited, turned on."

"Are you self-conscious at all?"

"Yes, very, but I want you to see me more than I want to hide myself, if that makes any sense."

I couldn't explain it any further as my thoughts and feelings were running through my head with such speed and desperation I could barely make sense of any of them. I should be horrified at my actions. I had stripped off my clothes for this man for nothing more than a cheap thrill, and I was standing in front of him, willing him to look at me.

"If I told you that the curtains on the far side of the room were hiding a window to the office next door, and I'm going to open them now so the staff working there can see you, how would you react?"

My clit spasmed with excitement at the idea of more people watching me and I could feel my juices running down the inside of my thighs. My hand made its way between my legs, and before I knew what I was doing I was playing with myself.

The therapist stood and walked to the other side off the room, where he pulled on a chord to open the curtains and reveal the office space behind them. He knocked on the window and a young man sitting behind a desk looked up and started speaking. I couldn't hear what he was saying, but two other men and a woman came into view, and they all moved toward the window, their eyes on me.

My fingers continued their movement against my clit and I moaned with pleasure. Every nerve ending in my body seemed to be on fire and I felt as if I was floating.

"Why don't you move over here and lean over the arm of the sofa so they can get a good look at your wet cunt?"

Having someone instruct me while others watched was adding a whole new dimension to my fantasy, only it wasn't a fantasy now: I was here, in this room, with a group of people watching me, and being told what to do by a complete stranger. The sensible part of my brain was still there and was screaming at me to stop, that this was not acceptable behavior in any way, shape or form, but it had become barely a whisper… a scratching at the back of my mind that was easily ignored.

I walked to the end of the sofa and bent over, shuffling my feet so my legs were apart to give them the best view possible. I couldn't see the window from this angle, but I didn't need to. I'd already seen them watching me, and my pussy was pulsating, desperate to be fucked for their viewing pleasure.

"Can I touch you?" Robert said. "Do you want me to participate or would that spoil your enjoyment?"

"Please…" I struggled to put the words together. "Please… yes… oh God…"

CHAPTER FOUR

He rested his hand on the small of my back, keeping it still for a moment, but it was enough to send a tremor of pleasure throughout my entire body. A low moan escaped my lips, and I was struggling to control my breathing.

"I need you to stay as still as possible, otherwise your audience won't be able to see you fully."

I nodded, and I grabbed one of the throw cushions so I had something to focus my energy on. His hand ran down my ass and my leg, all the way to my knee, before he slowly moved it back up to the inside of my thigh. I bit into the cushion and held my breath, waiting for his fingers to reach my pussy.

"You are so wet right now," Robert said. "I haven't even reached your pussy and my fingers are already covered in your juices, and I can see that your pussy is swollen and desperate to be fucked."

"Oh, God, yes! Please fuck me!" I shouted, and my words became lost in screams as his fingers found my clit and I fell headfirst into a raging orgasm. My legs were shaking and I fought to keep them still as my muscles shook and spasmed, but Robert didn't stop. He pushed a finger into my throbbing pussy, followed by another and another, and he found my g-spot and send me toppling into a second orgasm before I'd fully come out of the first one.

I'd never felt this level of pleasure before, and I was so lost in how my body was feeling that I'd forgotten why it was happening. Then Robert removed his fingers and pulled me into a standing position, and I remembered the people behind the window.

The woman and one of the men had left the room, but the other two men were seated behind their desks, and I could see their arms moving as they rubbed their cocks with excitement.

Robert pulled me around to the back of the sofa and bent me over again. I heard the rip of a condom packet, and the zip of his trousers being undone, and then he grabbed my hair in his fist and used it to turn my head to face the screen.

He entered me forcefully, and my hips pounded against the cold leather as he thrust into me. The men in the window stared at me as my therapist fucked me as hard as he could, and I could see by the looks on their faces, they were both close to coming.

One of them opened his mouth as his hand movements became faster, and then he slowed and let his head fall back against his chair. The other man was still frantically mastur-bating, and he seemed torn between scrunching his eyes closed to enjoy the sensation and not wanting to miss a moment of what was happening in the next room.

Robert reached a hand around my hips and rubbed his fingers

against my clit as he fucked me, and my body and mind began tumbling towards yet another orgasm. I let it flow over me, giving up any hope of control as my body convulsed around Robert's cock, and I stared at the man through the window the whole time.

He gave up trying to keep his eyes open and his entire face screwed up tight as he came, and then he seemed slightly embarrassed as he glanced over at the other man and shuffled out of his seat to leave the room.

I was past caring about other people's embarrassment, or my own, and even after Robert found his release, and tidied himself up, I remained where I was. My body was tingling from head to foot and my head was fuzzy. I giggled at the absurdity of what had just happened.

"There is a shower in the bathroom to the side if you want to freshen up," he said, motioning to a door on the opposite wall to the window. "And when you are ready we'll review the session."

I smiled at him, and fumbled my way to the bathroom, and once I'd set the shower to the right temperature and climbed under the spray, he opened the door and placed my clothes on a chair in the corner.

"Take your time," he said. "Come and join me when you're finished."

The water was warm and soothing, and I helped myself to the range of toiletries on the shelf. By the time I was finished I smelled of soap and honey, and my skin glistened with moisturizing oils. My legs were beginning to find their strength again, and I dried myself with an oversized super-soft towel and slipped into my clothes.

Robert was sitting at his desk, scribbling away in a notebook as I made my way back into the room and took a seat on the sofa. He'd obviously given it a wipe down as there was sign that anything sexual had happened. I took a mouthful of water and allowed him to finish what he was doing, not sure where this session was going next.

"What are your thoughts on what happened here this afternoon?" he asked, as he closed the book and took the seat opposite me.

"I don't know. I guess at least I know now there's definitely something wrong with me."

Now I was fully dressed again and regaining my faculties, I was starting to feel embarrassed about what I'd done, and I played my scarf around my fingers as I always did when I was nervous.

"Why do you think there's something wrong with you?"

"Isn't it obvious? What I did, that's not normal behavior, is it?"

"It depends what you think of as normal. You have a fetish, nothing more. Lots of people do, and lots of people hide those fetishes because they don't understand them. You like to be watched, and there is nothing at all wrong with that."

"But it is wrong. I mean, I can't simply go out exposing myself to people."

"Of course not. But that is what we need to work on rather

than trying to rid you of something that give you so much pleasure. You need to find a way to control how you enjoy this fetish rather than trying to prevent it, so that the people you expose yourself to are willing participants, and so that you are safe."

Robert stood and walked over to the curtains and drew them back to show the window where the office workers had been watching from. As the curtains parted, the office came into view and a man was sitting behind a desk talking, and as he knocked on the glass, two other men and a woman came into view. It was exactly the same as when he opened the curtains the first time.

"This is a recording," he said. "It gave you the illusion you were being watched by complete strangers when you were in fact not. You got to play out your fantasy while remaining perfectly safe."

I let out a self-conscious laugh, but I was also relieved that I hadn't made as big of a fool out of myself as I thought I had.

"I wanted to see how far you would go and what sort of control you had over yourself, in order to figure out the best way to help you. And now we know that this is something you need in order to be fully satisfied rather than something your simply curious about, I think I have something that would suit you perfectly."

Robert reached into his jacket pocket, pulled out a glossy business card, and handed it to me. It was all black, apart from the name KinkCorp written in silver, and a telephone number.

"Mistress Ellen runs an exclusive club not far from here, and while she doesn't normally take on new clients, I'm sure she'll be more than happy to help you find your feet."

"I don't understand. Aren't you going to fix me? Isn't that what you do?"

"It is what I do, but you don't need fixing. You need to learn to accept yourself with all your wonderful quirks. And Mistress Ellen will give you the ways and means to do that with a fully vetted audience and complete anonymity. I'll contact her this evening so expect a call tomorrow."

He stood, and held out a hand to me. I shook it, which seemed very formal given his cock had been inside be less than an hour before, but then this whole afternoon had been surreal. As we got to the foyer, he opened the door for me to leave, but stopped me briefly.

"My door is always open if you need me, although you'll be in good hands, so I doubt you will. But please, drop me an email just to let me know how you get on, will you?"

I nodded and thanked him. I didn't know if I would go through with meeting Mistress Ellen, but at least I felt more in control than I had in a long time.

BODY IMAGE

"I can't believe you're doing this for me, Kali. Thank you!"

Ryan held the door open and waved his arm around as an invitation for me to enter his studio.

"I'm glad to help, but you have to promise to paint me in a good light."

We'd been friends since high school sophomore year when we'd taking fine art together, so when he called me up to say he'd likely fail his college class because his model had dropped out at the last minute, I agreed to stand in without really thinking about it.

Now I was here, and things were about to get real, my nerves were kicking in.

"I've got everything set up ready, and if you want to take a break, just let me know and we'll stop."

There was a chaise lounge in the middle of the room draped with white satin sheets and surrounded with vases of lilies. I walked around it and sniffed one of the flowers, trying to buy a little time, as the reality of stripping off in front of him had me on the verge of a panic attack.

"Are you sure you can't get anyone else to do this?" I made a beeline for the small kitchen in the corner of the room. "I mean, this is awkward, right? You and me, and I'm not exactly model material."

Ryan picked up on my anxiety as he always did, and he met me in the kitchen and put some coffee on while trying to dispel my fear.

"We've been friends since school, and I like to think I know you almost as well as I know myself at this point." He grabbed two mugs from the cupboard and placed them in front of the coffee machine. "I know you have body image issues, so I was surprised when you agreed to model for me, and I want you to know that I asked you because I think you're beautiful and perfect and everything I need in a model." He fussed around adding sugar and milk to the mugs. "And yeah, this is crazy awkward because we're friends, but I promise you I'll be the perfect gentleman."

He pulled a stupid face and I laughed, a part of my fear dissipating. Ryan had always been a perfect gentleman, and that he felt the need to reassure and relax me was a great example.

We chatted for a while as we drank our coffee, and when my cup was empty I placed it on the counter top, took a deep breath, and walked over to the chaise lounge.

"Okay, let's do this before I change my mind."

I undid the buttons on my shirt dress, slipped it from my shoulders, and placed it on the desk by the window. Then I unhooked my bra and removed my panties as quickly as I could before placing my arms over my breasts and pussy and sitting down.

"You know I'm going to have to see you if I'm going to paint you, right?" Ryan walked over to me and squatted down. "Lie back and place your hands above your head, and bend your left knee so that your foot is level with your right knee, then drop your right leg off the side."

"Like this?" I did what I thought he wanted, but the frown on his face said otherwise.

"Can I?" He moved his hands toward me, and I nodded.

I could feel my skin flushing with embarrassment as he manipulated my arms and legs into his required position, and then out of nowhere, I felt a sudden surge of arousal. My skin became sensitive to his touch, and when he leaned over me to move my arms and his shirt brushed across my breasts, my nipples hardened. All I could focus on was his touch… and his scent. It was musky and warm with a hint of sweetness, and it seemed to cloak me, caressing every part of my body.

What the hell was this? I'd never noticed the way he smelled before, let alone been turned on by it, and I'd never thought of him as anything other than one of my best friends, so why was I suddenly getting aroused by him?

I told myself off mentally, and I reminded myself that I didn't normally strip naked and allow Ryan, or anyone else for that matter, to manhandle me whichever way he wanted, and the reaction I was having was nothing more than my mind desperately trying to make sense of the situation, and to distract me from the fact I was flaunting my overweight naked body in broad daylight.

He finished positioning me and stood back to make sure everything was as he wanted, and I couldn't help but notice his erection. He was wearing jogging bottoms, and his cock was forcing the front of them outward. He saw me staring and looked down.

"I'm sorry, Kali. I can't control it." He moved behind the easel and picked up a paint brush. "But please take it as a compliment. It doesn't stand to attention for just anyone. Now hold that position, and if you do need to move, let me know first."

I*t doesn't stand to attention for just anyone.* Those words played over and over in my head as I laid on the chaise lounge, completely naked with my arms above my head and my legs apart. Did he really find my body attractive?

All I saw when I looked in the mirror was breasts too large, a stomach that wobbled, hips that were far too wide, and thighs that chafed when I walked, and I couldn't comprehend how anyone could look at all that and think it attractive. Yes, I'd dated, and yes, I'd had sex, but it was always with the lights out and the covers up, and even then I'd been too self-conscious to really let myself enjoy the situation. If I was being honest, every sexual encounter I'd had was because I thought it was expected of me rather than for my own enjoyment.

I stared at the ceiling to avoid making eye contact with him, and my mind played that moment over and over. I saw Ryan standing over me, his erection standing proud. I saw the muscles in his arms ripple as he worked, and his dark hair flopping over his forehead as he bent forward. I saw his green eyes staring at my body, and the corners of his lips turning into a half-smile. I saw line of hair between his jogging bottoms and his belly button as his tshirt lifted, and the hint of well-defined muscles underneath his tanned skin.

I saw…

I suddenly realized that the reason I'd never been attracted to Ryan was because I didn't allow myself to see him. I was too afraid of rejection to allow myself to even think along those lines with him. But if he thought of me as beautiful, maybe… I had nothing else to do than get lost in my own thoughts, and now he dominated all of them.

In my mind, Ryan placed my arms over my head, and I took a deep breath, taking his scent into my lungs. He looked down at me, his eyes filled with need, and he ran his fingers down my wrists, elbows, shoulders. Gooseflesh followed in their wake, and sparks of arousal shot through my core as he played across my breasts.

My breathing became heavier, and I blinked, trying to pull myself away from those thoughts without moving. I could already feel a faint thudding behind my clit, and the coolness of the breeze over my pussy left me in no doubt that I was wet down there. I glanced at Ryan to see if he'd noticed, but thankfully, he seemed too caught up in his artwork to pay me any attention.

I needed to get my mind off him somehow, although with nothing else to do other than think, it was going to be hard. I recited the alphabet backward in my head, and then I tried to name an animal for each letter. I counted down from one hundred in groups of three and ran through half a dozen multiplication tables.

I was trying to remember the capital cities of countries around the world when his voice distracted me, and I was suddenly back to having him leaning over me. He was whispering in my ear about how he wanted to kiss my breasts and thrust his fingers inside me to feel my wetness, and I moaned quietly as he spoke.

"Kali, are you with me?"

Yes, I was, completely and utterly with him, and I arched my back, lifting my breasts to his waiting mouth.

"Kali, I said I'm finished for now."

Oh God! Reality came crashing down around me. He was standing by the easel with a grin on his face, and I could feel my entire body flush with embarrassment.

"I… um…" I scrambled up into a sitting position and looked around for my clothes.

After handing me a robe, Ryan walked to kitchen area and poured two glasses of iced water. I turned to look out of the window instead of making eye contact with him, and I chastised myself for thinking about him in the way I had. He was my best friend, for God's sake, and I was pretty sure I'd made him feel uncomfortable, even if he wasn't showing it.

"Do you want to take a look?" I jumped as the warm air from his words tickled the back of my ear. He held a glass out to me and tilted his head. "I still need to add some detail, but the basic image is there."

I followed him across the room to the easel, and I scrunched my face up, mentally preparing myself to see a hideously fat woman sprawled in a sexual way, but I was completely unprepared for the image on the canvas.

It was definitely me. My face was the same, my hair, and even the birthmark on my outer thigh. The position was the same as well, but the woman in the painting had soft, radiant-looking skin, large but perfectly rounded breasts, a full, smooth stomach, and perfectly proportioned hips and thighs. Instead of looking like she was offering herself up for sex, she looked confident in her own skin and comfortable with the rest of the world seeing her at her most vulnerable. I didn't know how to respond, and I stood there holding my breath as I took in every part of the painting.

"What do you think?" He was standing behind me and I could feel his body heat searing into my skin. A sudden unexpected feeling of anger coursed through me, and I turned to face him.

"What do I think? Seriously? You had me come here and take my clothes off, knowing how I feel about myself, and you use me as nothing more than an outline to paint another woman's body? Why would you do that?" I glared at him as I pulled my robe tighter, and he responded with a look of confusion.

"I don't understand, Kali. What other woman?" I laughed and strode off to find my clothes, but he grabbed my arm and forced me to face the canvas. "Can you really not see that this is you?"

"Of course it's not me. Look at her. She's so…"

"Strong? Beautiful? Perfect?"

"Yes. She is nothing like me." Tear were welling up in my eyes, and I blinked hard and fast to try to keep them under control.

"She is you, Kali. I told you I thought you were beautiful, and this is what I see when I look at you, can't you understand that? I know you see yourself as fat, but I see a body I could wrap myself around without breaking. I see breasts I want to bury my face in for all eternity. I see hips I could grab as I lose myself inside you. And I see you, inside that body; intelligent, radiant, strong, sensitive, and yes, perfect."

The tears finally escaped, and I brushed them away with my fingers as Ryan gazed at the painting.

"Why haven't you said any of this before?"

"Why? Because you made it clear when we first met that you weren't interested in me. I can't imagine the world without you as a part of it, and I wasn't going to risk losing you just so I could get my feelings off my chest. But you need to hear this now, for your sake. You need to hear that you are so much more beautiful than you could ever admit to, because you are missing out on so much by hating yourself."

I turned to face him, my eyes blurry and my cheeks burning, and I wrapped myself around his torso and pulled him tight against me. He cocooned me in his arms and buried his head in my shoulder, and I don't know how it happened, but the next thing I knew my lips were against his.

CHAPTER FOUR

H e tasted of coffee and mint as he thrust his tongue into my mouth, and I responded with my own tongue playing against his. My body tingled with desire, and for the first time, I didn't feel the need to run away or hide myself. Before I could second guess myself, I reached down, undid the fastenings on the robe, and let it fall to the floor.

Ryan stood back and took a deep breath as his eyes wandered over my body. "Are you sure you want this?"

I didn't answer him. Instead, I smiled, took hold of his hand, and placed it on my breast. He groaned as his fingers touched my skin, and his cock grew hard, straining against the fabric of his joggers. I took hold of the bottom of his tshirt and lifted it over his head, and then I ran my fingers around the elastic waistband of his joggers and eased it over his cock.

His hand stayed still on my breast, and I faltered, that ingrained doubt raising its head again, but then he spoke.

"I promised you I'd be the perfect gentleman."

"Did you mean it when you said you wanted me?" I took his cock in my hand and ran my fingers over it. He sucked in air and nodded. "Then wouldn't it be the gentlemanly thing to do to give me what I want?"

"What do you want?" His hand moved to cup my breast, and his thumb brushed over my nipple.

I swallowed and used the most confident voice I could muster. "You say you think I'm beautiful. Show me."

He made a guttural sound deep in his throat and stared into my eyes for a moment, before pushing the furniture away from the middle of the room and laying a blanket down in the space. He held out a hand and I walked to him and took it, and I let him lower me to the floor, his eyes never leaving mine.

"You have the most perfect face. Your eyes are alert and inquisitive, your high cheekbones and straight nose pull attention to your full lips, that are both pouty and cheeky at the same time." He lowered himself over me and kissed both my eyelids, followed by my cheeks and nose, and then he kissed my lips with that perfect mouth of his.

He trailed the kiss down my chin and neck, and over my shoulders, and then he sat up.

"Where to start on your breasts. Even under clothing, I was mesmerized by them. You have no idea how many times I've had to stop myself from reaching out and touching them, and to see them like this and knowing I can touch them," he ran the fingers of both hands lightly over my breasts, and I arched my back as gooseflesh erupted over my skin, "If the world were to end right now, I would go out the happiest man on earth."

His mouth worked its way over one of my breasts, kissing in circles that slowly reduced in size until he took one of my nipples in his mouth. He sucked it in and ran his tongue around it, and a bolt of pleasure shot straight to my clit as his teeth grazed over my hardened bud.

My enjoyment must have been obvious as he lifted his head and grinned before repeating everything on my other breast, and by the time he turned his attention to my stomach, I was lost in his touch.

"I know you hate this part of you. I know you think you need to lose weight, but I love that there is enough of you to grab hold of, and enough for me to kiss and suck and bite."

He spoke against my stomach, the heat from his mouth searing my skin, and after each word he butterflied kisses from one side to the other, and he dipped his tongue into my belly button as he passed it, sending shivers deep into my flesh.

"And this part. I always imagined seeing you like this one day, but no amount of imagination prepared me for seeing your pussy in all its glory." He ran both his hands over my hips and mound before using his thumbs to open me up. "Your neatly trimmed hair hides your perfect pink folds, but when you open your legs it's like an orchid unfolding for the sun. Your wetness glistens like tiny diamonds, and when I spread your folds wide, your clit peeks out from under its hood, calling to me to play with it."

Ryan lowered his head, and I let out a moan as his tongue slipped over my clit. All my anxiety and self-hatred melted away completely in that moment, and I closed my eyes and allowed myself to truly feel my own arousal.

Ryan's tongue lapped and circled my clit, and I stretched my arms above my head, reveling in the feeling. I'd never let anyone see me down there, let alone pleasure me, and I was now realizing what I'd been missing out on.

The coolness of the air mixed with the heat from his mouth in swirls, and every stroke against my clit caused a trembling through my core. Pressure began building deep inside me, and I relaxed into the feeling as his mouth worked its way over my pussy.

It wasn't long before the pressure turned into a ball of heat and desperation, and it released in an explosion of muscle spasms and screams. My pussy pulsed so strongly it felt as if it would rip apart, and he pushed his tongue inside me, drinking down my juices as they flowed from my opening.

As my orgasm ebbed, Ryan kissed his way back up to my mouth and gave me my first taste of myself. I devoured my juices on his lips and tongue, and when we came up for air, he gazed into my eyes with such love my heart melted.

"Have I convinced you how amazing you are yet?" He brushed a strand of hair from my face as he spoke.

"Almost." I lay there underneath him, marveling at how me made me feel.

"Almost? How can I get you to definitely?"

I smiled and lifted my head to kiss him. "You can make love to me."

"Are you sure? I mean, oh God, yes, I want to! But are you absolutely sure?"

I nodded and kissed him again, and he wrapped his arms around me and nuzzled into my neck before jumping up and backing away toward the bedroom door.

"Don't go anywhere, okay?"

He disappeared from view for a moment, and when he returned he had a pack of condoms with him. I hadn't even considered protection. All I wanted was him inside me, and all other thoughts were out of my grasp, but luckily one of us had our wits about us.

He kneeled on the blanket, took a packet from the box, and ripped it open with his teeth. I watched as he pumped his cock in his hand a few times and applied the condom to the tip, rolling it carefully down his length. When it was in place, he crawled back over me and positioned himself at my opening.

"I can't believe this is finally happening." He stayed motionless for a minute. "I've thought about this moment since the first time I met you." And then he thrust forward slowly and entered me.

CHAPTER SIX

He kept eye contact as he filled me, and I lifted my hips to meet him. He felt so good, as if he belonged inside me, and I wrapped my legs around his back as he began thrusting into me.

I could feel every inch of him as he moved, his thick cock rubbing against my pussy walls, stimulating my g-spot. His chest rubbed against my breasts as he thrusted, and my nipples hardened against him, enjoying the attention.

His speed increased, and I could feel myself at the beginning of another orgasm, something I hadn't believed possible through penetration alone. My breathing became faster as it built inside me, and I was pretty sure Ryan wasn't far off either, as his forehead furrowed in concentration.

"I'm going to come." I gasped. "Come with me."

He paused, then shook his head and grinned before increasing his thrusts, and it wasn't long before I was panting and moaning, my inner muscles clamping down hard around his cock.

"Oh fuck, you feel so good." His face contorted into a look that could have been construed as agony if he were doing anything else, and he rammed his cock into me as fast as he could before stopping deep inside me. I could feel him coming. His cock pulsed, emptying his seed into the condom, and my pussy muscles responded, milking him for every last drop.

When he was finished, he sank down on top of my and buried his head in my neck, his breathing harsh and fast, and I felt rather than heard the words "I love you" as they vibrated against my skin.

I stroked his hair, his shoulders, his back, his cock still inside me, and as it softened I tightened my pussy muscles, trying to keep him in place. When he finally slipped from inside me, he rolled over, removed the condom, and wrapped his arms around me.

We laid together, wrapped in each other's arms, enjoying the closeness in silence, and I replayed the afternoon in my head. I never thought I'd have the courage to show my body in front of any man until now, but with Ryan it had been easy, and the words he'd spoken into my neck…

"Did you mean what you said?"

He shifted his position, creating space between us so he could turn onto his side and look at me. "Every word of it."

"No, I mean that last thing. After you came." Tears trickled down my cheeks as I waited for his response.

"You mean when I said I love you?" He ran his fingers down my cheek, tracing the line of my tears, and smiled. "Kali

McDonald, I love you. You have no idea just how much I love you."

My tears turned into a flood, and he held me tight as I broke against his chest.

"I love you too." I'd expected the first time I uttered those words to be far more romantic and not during a complete emotional breakdown, but every expectation I'd had to this point had just been completely demolished, so I wasn't going to let a little thing like dignity stand in my way.

He kissed my tears away, first one cheek, then the other, and then my nose, and my lips, and only after he'd had his fill of me did he speak.

"It's turning dark. You could go home now, or I could phone for some takeout and we can replay everything in the bedroom. Then in the morning, you could go back to your place and pack your things up and come back."

"You mean move in here? With you?"

"Why not? It might not have been sexual until today, but we've been in a relationship for three years, and honestly, I don't want to waste another minute pretending we aren't meant for each other."

It was a crazy idea. A few hours ago we were best friends and nothing else. But it felt right, and I didn't want to waste another minute either.

"Thai."

"Tie what?"

"If you're ordering out. I fancy Thai"

DEN OF INIQUITY

"You were hard to track down, Genevieve." Athelina ran a hand across a rack of whips in the corner of the room. "We expected to see the usual spike in deaths in the area, so you can imagine our surprise when not only was there not, but we find you living amongst humans as one of them."

I read the business card the succubus had given me on entering my office and took a deep breath. "The arrangement suits me. I'm not a cause for concern, so what does the International Council want with me?"

Athelina smiled and took a seat at the desk opposite me. "As you are aware, the past few decades have been very different to the ones before. With the invention of the internet, we are no longer able to keep under the radar as we used to. The destruction of a small village in the middle of nowhere is now reported globally, and we've had instances of feeding by certain breeds caught on film. We've been able to debunk them so far, but increased surveillance by the humans is putting us all at risk."

"I don't understand what this has to do with me." I poured a glass of water, my throat dry with nerves, and I offered a glass to Athelina.

"No, thank you." She leaned forward, her eyes fixed on mine. "What it has to do with you is that you've achieved what none of us have been able to. Assimilation. We want to learn from you, to know how you've managed to feed without drawing any attention whatsoever, and how you manage to pass as one of them."

"What I do might work for succubae, but I can't see it working for the other breeds." I took a sip of the water and shuffled in my seat uncomfortably.

"It's more than we have right now, and the survival of one breed is better than none, is it not?" She leaned back and crossed one long, slim leg over the other. "I will spend some time with you, and you can show me what you've accomplished. Is that acceptable to you?"

I wanted to tell her to go to hell, that she was risking everything I had for no other reason than short-sightedness on the part of others, but I'd had dealings with the Council over the centuries and I knew they wouldn't take no for an answer.

"It's acceptable, but there have to be terms attached."

"What sort of terms?"

"You do as I say. If I tell you to stop, you do. And if I see anyone's life put at risk because of your actions, I will demand that you leave." I stared back at her, letting her know that I was serious and hoping she didn't spot my body trembling at the thought of standing up to her. She placed her hands together and steepled her fingers under her chin, seemingly deep in thought for a moment. Then a half-smile appeared on her face, and she stood.

"I accept your terms. Where do we start?"

"My guests will be arriving around eight this evening. I can get someone to show you to a guest room if you haven't arranged accommodation."

"That is very generous of you, Genevieve."

I phoned through to my assistant and asked her to escort Athelina to the east wing suite, and I stood and shook her hand with a pasted smile on my face.

As soon as I was alone, I slumped back into my chair, threw my head back, and screamed silently into the air. I had trained myself to live around humans, but an untrained succubus staying under the same roof as my guests posed a huge threat, and I would have to be vigilant until I could get her to leave.

The clock on the fireplace chimed six times, dragging me from my thoughts, and I pulled myself together and headed to my quarters to prepare for my weekend guests.

CHAPTER TWO

I checked myself over in the full-length mirror to make sure I looked the part. Black leather thigh-high stiletto boots, thong and bra showed off my toned, sun-bronzed body, and my dark hair, pulled up in a high ponytail, accentuated my neck and shoulders. I applied crimson gloss to my lips and smoky black liner to my eyes, and I smiled at the end result. Perfection as always.

I'd almost forgotten about the guest in the east wing, and I was busy doing a final safety check on the equipment when she walked in.

"You didn't tell me you were having a fancy dress party, Genevieve. I'd have dressed up if I'd known."

"That's Mistress Genevieve to you." I may have been nervous about her presence earlier, but I was in dominatrix mode now, and if Athelina wanted to be here, she would damn well fall in line. "I'll get the waiting staff to rustle up another uniform for you. You will serve drinks, and you will observe. That is all. Do you understand?"

"Actually no, I don't. What is all this? And I'm already famished so I would like you to show me how you feed."

"This, dear Athelina, is my very own den of iniquity as you would likely call it, and you will be well fed, just not in the way you are accustomed to. Now do as you're told and stop asking questions, or I'll have to punish you. And trust me when I say this; I will enjoy every minute of it."

The sudden ring of the doorbell forced my attention away, and I waved a hand at her. "Go, now." She stood and gave me a look of defiance for a moment before she realized this was exactly what she'd agreed to and nodded in submission. "That's it. Good girl. Charlotte, take Athelina to the dressing room and find her an outfit, please."

As the waitress ushered Athelina out of the room, I turned my attention to the newly arrived guests. Stephen, his wife Janine, and a woman I didn't recognize sauntered into the room, and I gave each of them a glowing smile and a warm hug.

"Janine, my darling, it's so good to see you, as it is you, Stephen. And who, pray tell, is your friend?" I caught that her name was Stephanie, but my main attention was on her excited energy. It flowed from her like a fountain, and I took a deep breath, tasting it as I welcomed her into the Manor House.

I'd feasted on both Stephen and Janine many times, and they were delicious, but the thought of new blood set my taste buds alight. I wondered if she'd be delicate and sweet or heavy and fulfilling as arousal coursed through her, and I made a mental note to find out exactly what she liked. I let them head in the direction of the changing area, and licked my lips, devouring the last of Stephanie's energy before it dissipated.

Through the large arched windows, I could see a car pulling up and a man getting out, and my pussy let out a little pulse of joy. Of all the guests that passed through the Manor House halls, Phillip was the one that interested me the most. He was tall, handsome in a rugged sort of way, and muscular to the point of distraction. He was everything people expect from a dominant alpha male, but instead of trying to take charge on our first meeting, he'd dropped to his knees and offered himself up to me for whatever I desired.

"Slave." I didn't smile or offer to hug him. Instead I placed one foot in front of the other and waited. He lowered his head and said, "It's good to see you, Mistress," before falling to his knees and taking my foot in his hands. Without instruction he lifted my boot to his face and licked from the pointed tip all the way to my knee. Seeing him beneath me, degrading himself for my pleasure, sent a spark of heat through my core, and my juices trickled down the inside of my thighs. He finished cleaning the leather and looked up.

"Would you like me to lick your thighs clean, Mistress? I can see how wet they are."

Another spark raced through me and my clit throbbed with need, but I knew I couldn't allow him to pleasure me this soon or I'd drain him before I could stop myself.

"Not now, slave. I have guests to attend to. Run along and have some fun. I'll find you when I'm ready for you."

The room was full, and people mingled and chatted, getting to know each other before the fun started. I spotted Athelina at the other end of the room paying far too much attention to one particular guest, and I made my way quickly in her direction and caught her arm.

"Can I see you in the kitchen for a moment."

"I'm fine where I am."

"That wasn't a request, and when I say in a moment, I mean now."

She followed obediently, and I breathed a sigh of relief. The last thing I needed was to monitor her all night, and although I'd warned my assistant to keep a close eye on her, I knew full well that if a succubus wanted to feed, there was little a human could do to stop them. I waited until the waitresses grabbed their trays and left the kitchen before turning to her.

"You cannot spend that amount of time with any one guest, do you hear?"

Athelina let out a huff. "I don't get what you're doing here. Is this your perverse idea of fun? And look at me! I look like a prostitute! And I'm starving. You said we'd feed."

She did look good in her waitress outfit that consisted of a short, flared black skirt to show of her legs and her bare ass as she leaned over to pick up glasses from the tables, and an under-bust corset that pushed her bare breasts up to enhance their shape. I'd picked the look myself, as not only did it provide me with a beautiful display, but it got the blood flowing in the majority of my clientele.

I leaned forward and cupped her breasts in my hands, and I took her nipples between my fingers and thumbs and squeezed. She gasped, and lifted her hands to push me away, but a single harsh look sent her hands back to her sides while I tortured her.

"Think of what is happening now as the appetizer, and we are in a full course restaurant. We taste every dish as it is served, but it is only a mouthful. We are left hungry to begin with, but in return we get to taste many dishes."

I lowered my head and took one of her nipples in my mouth, sucking in in and nibbling with just enough pressure to hurt. She groaned and ran her fingers through my ponytail as I moved to her other nipple.

"Once you've had a taste of one human, you move on to the next, do you understand?" I spoke between licks and bites, and she mumbled her understanding between gasps and moans.

"If you follow my instructions, not only will you get to taste each and every course, but I promise you will have a most pleasurable night."

I slipped a hand between her legs and thrust two fingers inside her as a promise of what she could gain from complying, and she whimpered and shuffled her feet apart. Her pussy was wet, and my fingers slid in and out with ease. My thumb found her clit and circled over it, sending shudders through her body, and her breathing became heavier. While her reaction was what I wanted, and her submission to me was welcome, I didn't trust that her hunger wouldn't take over and destroy everything I'd worked for.

"If you seriously want to know how I've flown under the radar for so long, please use this time to watch. You never know, you may not only learn a few things, but you may come to appreciate the humans you look down on."

I removed my hand and left her in a state of frustration in the kitchen to think about what I'd said, and I hoped at least some of it had sunk in, otherwise I could kiss goodbye to the Manor House and everything I'd built around it.

The pleasantries were over and done with, and I took to the stage. "Welcome everyone, old and new. I know this is the part of the night you've all been waiting for, so to kick us off I'd like to welcome the amazing Kiki DeVine to the stage to show you how not to prepare your vegetables for a wholesome family meal, and for those interested in a more hands-on approach, the wall of pain is now officially open."

The crowd erupted in a round of applause, and some took their seat for the show while others eagerly headed for the back of the room. Kiki kicked off her act by slicing the end off a zucchini, placing it upright on a chair, and saying "Now you see it..." before squatting onto the vegetable and standing up again. "Now you don't, and that's magic."

I wandered through the laughing crowd, breathing in the sweet, subtle sexual energy they emitted, and although it tasted good, after my encounter with Athelina I was ready for a larger meal.

The first of the submissives had been handcuffed to the 'wall of pain', and I made my way to the area to check that the rules were being followed. It was rare that anyone took advantage, and for the most part, the subs controlled the narrative. If they were being punished, it was because they wanted to be. They'd purposely broken a rule they'd set in order to receive a spanking or a whipping from their doms. It was fascinating to watch, and it had taken me a while to understand that while the doms appeared to be the ones in charge, it was the subs that held all the power in the relationship.

The sexual energy was stronger here, a mixture of excited expectation and desperate need, and I thought about taking my fill from them, but I wanted Athelina to understand how simple it is to feed without harm. She was hanging back behind the bar, closing in on the staff, but they were well-trained and wouldn't provide her with anywhere near the energy she needed. I caught her eye and motioned for her to join me.

"No more than a breath or two from each person. Understood?" I waited for her to nod her agreement, and then walked her through the guests who were enjoying the scene playing out in front of them.

I held my own breath and watched as she moved through the group. Her chest expanded as she passed each person, and her skin flushed as she fed, and then she stopped, her attention on the wall in front of her.

Her eyes widened as she watched a young woman squirm with pleasure as an older man sent a leather flogger stinging against her large breasts over and over, and she seemed to forget her reason for being there.

Her own bare breasts flushed with excitement, and her

nipples hardened. It was very rare indeed for a succubus to let go of any level of perceived control, but Athelina's body language screamed submissive in that moment, and my lips widened into a smile as I contemplated the fun I could have with her later. But for now, it was important to keep her moving and feeding. I checked my watch and ran my hand down her arm to break her focus.

"Carry on working your way to the end of the group, then follow me."

CHAPTER FIVE

The relaxation room, as the guests had named it, was beginning to fill up, and that was where the main course took place. I waited for Athelina to join me by the door and I handed her a tray of champagne glasses.

"How is your appetite after that little show?"

"It definitely took the edge off my hunger, but it's not going to sustain me for long. Do you really survive like this?" She was looking around the main hall, still not fully understanding what I was doing, but she would very shortly.

"You'll have your fill through this door, providing you continue to follow my instruction. I want you to place a glass of champagne next to each guest and remove any empty glasses they've left. You get to feed off each person for exactly the amount of time it takes to do that, no more."

She gave me a questioning look, and she smiled when I opened the door and allowed her to see what was on the other side.

The guests were already in full flow. Clothes were placed in neat piles on the shelves in the corner of the room, and naked bodies writhed on the mattresses that filled the floor. The sexual energy was potent in this room, and I took a deep breath, filling myself with their essence.

Athelina didn't wait for further instruction, and she moved into the room, bending down by each person and feeding while she placed a glass next to them. The guests barely registered she was there, as they lost themselves in their need for each other.

A middle-aged woman lay on her back with her legs spread wide, and she moaned and whimpered as her partner ran his tongue over her clit. The man lying next to her leaned over and took one of her nipples in his mouth while his wife's head was bobbing up and down as she sucked on his hard cock. Another man was thrusting his cock in and out of her wet pussy as she sucked, his motions making her breasts move like large pendulums.

There was more than enough energy coming from this one grouping to satiate even the hungriest succubus without doing any permanent damage to the humans, but the trick was to take a little from each so they were not even aware they were food.

Once she'd placed a glass by each of the five participants, Athelina moved on to the next group of people. Five or six men and women surrounded a single woman in the middle of the group, and as I took a closer look, I recognized the new woman Janine and Stephen had brought with them. Her arms and legs were splayed and held in place as the others feasted on her body. One woman thrust fingers in and out of her pussy while a man licked her clit, two men knelt either side, kneading her breasts and sucking on her nipples, and another woman straddled her face. Stephanie groaned and strained her neck to push her tongue into the offered pussy while her body rippled with orgasmic contractions, and I was glad to find out I'd been right about her, as the essence coming from her was more powerful than I'd tasted in a very long time.

Again, Athelina did as she was told and spent no more time with the group than it took to replenish their drinks, even though they were far more tempting to stay near than the others. She made her way around the rest of the room, and fed from a woman with a cock in every hole, a man with a cock pounding his ass while his own came in another person's mouth, and two women who were lost in pleasuring each other with vibrators while their lips locked and their tongues entwined.

I followed her, taking sips from each rather than fully feeding so as not to drain them too much, and once we'd had our fill, we left the inhabitants of the room to continue their pleasuring of each other in peace.

"I honestly didn't know what to expect this evening," Athelina said as she placed the empty tray on the end of the bar. "I thought you'd created this place to find a specific type of person to feed from, you know, a deviant who wouldn't be missed, but this is ingenious."

"I'm glad you've enjoyed it. As you can see, we never have to go hungry and no human is hurt in the process." I ran a finger down her cheek and brushed a stray strand of hair behind her ear. "And there is an additional bonus to feeding like this."

Her forehead scrunched and she tilted her head, trying to work out what I could possibly mean.

"Let me ask you this, Athelina. Have you ever had sex with a human where the purpose of it was enjoyment not sustenance?"

"Of course not. What would be the point in that?" The confusion in her face gave way to distain, and I laughed aloud.

"I would have said the same many moons ago, but it turns out, when our bellies are full and we can instead concentrate on our own bodies, a human mate can bring us pleasure at a level I've never felt before." I looked around the room, searching for two specific people, and when I spotted them I whispered to one of the staff to have them escorted to my suite.

Athelina was still giving me that look, and I had no doubt she would have retired to her room if I'd left her, but I wanted her to experience this evening in full, and instead I took her by the hand and led her through the room to the stairs before she could argue with me.

CHAPTER SIX

I poured a glass of sparkling water for each of us while we waited for our company, and Athelina moved through my private rooms, running her hands over my collection of whips and toys.

"I don't understand why you enjoy this. I can see after this evening why humans feel the need to play these games, but surely we are above this. We are hunters not prey, after all."

"I've watched you this evening, and you are not as 'above this' as you think you are." There was a knock on the door and I smiled at Athelina as I let our guests in. "And not only are you 'not above' this, but I've a feeling you are about to learn about a side of your personality you never knew existed."

Phillip lowered his head as he walked past me to take his place next to the bed, but he couldn't contain the excited grin that spread across his face. I pretended not to see it, as I would have to punish him for his impertinence, and I wanted to give my attention to our other guest to make sure he knew what was expected of him.

Like Phillip, Saul was tall and muscular and oozed masculinity, but unlike Phillip, he was not about to become anyone's plaything. Saul was the epitome of dominance, and I shook my head as he moved toward me and pointed at Athelina.

"She's new to the scene, and she needs a firm hand to teach her." I opened a set of double doors to reveal a smaller version of the wall in the main hall, complete with metal rings, chains and cuffs, and an large array of toys and tools.

Saul tested the wall restraints and ran his hand over the display of tools, and he turned to Athelina and smiled. "You look like a fighter. Do I have your consent?"

Athelina huffed and opened her mouth to tell him where to go, but her chest was already flushed, and her excitement was visible on her inner thighs as her juices glistened against her skin. She wanted this, even if she wouldn't admit it, and she couldn't bring herself to walk away.

"Fine. You have my consent. But don't think you can dominate me. I don't submit to meagre beings like you."

"Suit yourself, but you may find I'm not so meagre, and you're more willing to submit than you think you are. Now pick a safe word."

"I don't need..."

"Everyone needs a safe word. Now pick one, even if you don't plan on using it."

She looked at him with the intent of getting him to back down, but he stared back in silence. "Okay, I'll go with 'food'." I gave her a glare, warning her to behave, and she shrugged her shoulders. "What? It's just a word, right?"

"Food it is then. If you want to stop at any time, just use that word. Now, let's get you warmed up, shall we?" Saul picked up a leather collar with a metal ring attached to it and placed it around her neck. "You're mine now. I own you, and I will do whatever I want with this luscious body of yours."

Athelina feigned annoyance, but her excitement was obvious to everyone in the room, and she allowed herself to be led to the wall, where her limbs were spread wide and attached with cuffs and chains to the secure rings. Once she was unable to move, Saul ran a final chain through the metal ring on the collar and attached it high up either side of her face to prevent her lowering her head.

With Athelina in good hands, I turned my attention to Phillip. He was kneeling by the side of the bed with his head down, quietly waiting for instruction. I ran my hand through his hair and grabbed it at the back, pulling his head up to face me.

"I'd like to get undressed now. And I could do with a bath while I watch the show."

He jumped to his feet and began undoing the fastenings on my bra. His hands were smooth and gentle, and he slipped the straps from my shoulders releasing my breasts. Then he dropped back to his knees and slid the zippers down on my boots before lifting each of my legs in turn and removing stilettoed leather from my feet. Finally, he moved around so his face was level with my hips, hooked his fingers into each side of my thong, and pulled it down my legs. He licked his lips at the sight of my glistening, naked pussy, but he didn't attempt to taste me, knowing that he was not allowed, at least not yet.

I stretched my arms above my head, relishing the feeling of my naked skin, before crawling onto the bed and propping myself up on my pillows to get a good look at the wall. Phillip started with my feet, he had a bit of a fetish for them, and as his tongue wound its way around my toes, I smiled.

Athelina also had a smile on her face. Now she was immobilized, her need for control had waned, and she was giving herself to the torment Saul was inflicting on her. Her breasts were already red from the lashings from the flogger, and she groaned as he gripped each breast in turn and secured a clamp on each nipple. Once they were in place, he stood back and hit them with the flogger, and Athelina cried out in painful pleasure with each strike.

I closed my eyes and listened to her as Phillips tongue made its way over my ankles and knees to my thighs, and I moaned contently as he skirted around my pussy to clean my stomach. The heat of his tongue with the coolness of the trail he left behind sent ripples of delight through my skin, and my pussy pulsed with anticipation.

He shifted on the bed, positioning himself over my hips, and he grabbed my breasts in his hands, his eager mouth finding my nipples and sucking and nibbling on them. Sparks of heat shot from my nipples to my clit, and my inner muscles spasmed with every brush of his teeth.

I opened my eyes again as Athelina's groans became louder, interested to see what Saul was doing to her. He had a vibrator placed against her clit, and he was flicking the nipple clamps with his thumb and finger. Her head was moving from side to side as much as the restraints would allow, and I could see her stomach muscles rippling beneath her skin.

She was on the verge of an orgasm, and the way her skin reddened in preparation was beautiful to watch, and then he ripped the clamps from her nipples, and she screamed as her orgasm released in a powerful series of convulsions.

I realized I was panting in unison with Athelina's screams, and I wasn't only getting turned on by Phillips tongue on my body but by the scene I was watching, and I decided to take advantage of this unusual position. I called Saul over and whispered in his ear. He nodded his agreement and walked back to the wall to undo the restraints.

Phillip was used to pleasuring me without any reciprocal pleasure, but tonight he was going to get my attention. I could hear Saul's voice telling Athelina what she had to do, and I made sure Phillip knew his part in the picture.

"I'm not doing that!" Athelina's voice pulled my attention to her.

"You'll do as you're told." She stepped away from the wall at Saul's voice and walked toward my bed. I gave her a raised eyebrow and a grin, and she glared in response, but she crawled between my legs anyway.

Her tongue to my clit sent sparks throughout my body, made all the better by knowing she was doing her best to pleasure me simply because her master had told her to. I squirmed under her attention for a few minutes, enjoying the focused attention, and then I motioned to Phillip to take his position.

He straddled my neck and presented his cock to my face, and I licked my lips and took his length into my mouth. Athelina's tongue became harsher, which let me know that Saul was fucking her from behind as she licked my clit, and I wrapped my tongue and lips around Phillip's cock encouraging him to face-fuck me as hard as he wanted.

When I came, it was harsh and visceral, and I pulled Phillip's cock from my mouth so I could scream and yell until the assault on my body eased and my muscle spasms became bearable again.

Once I started to come down from my orgasm, I sucked Phillip's cock back into my mouth and played with him until he came, squirting his cum down my throat. His pleasure was almost as important as my own, and I drank him down enthusiastically as proof of my power over him.

CHAPTER EIGHT

Athelina's tongue was no longer on my clit, but I was too wrapped up in my own post-orgasmic glow to care about what she was doing or whether her or Saul had reached their peak. I rolled over on my stomach, blocking my guests from any further access to my body, and I stretched out and closed my eyes.

I don't know how long I'd been lying there when Athelina's voice brought me back. Both Phillip and Saul had left, knowing when their presence was no longer required, but Athelina was new to this world and was obviously in need of some reassurance.

I allowed her to crawl in bed beside me, and I caressed her hair as she wrapped her limbs around my body.

"So, do you understand the lure of human sexuality now?"

"I agree that there is a certain something to enjoying sex for the sake of sex."

"A 'certain something'?" I laughed, remembering her moaning

and panting as Saul teased and tormented her, and how she screamed out her orgasm as it tore through her body and mind. Her cheeks were turning a lovely shade of red, and she averted her eyes from mine.

"Okay, I admit, it was extremely enjoyable, and I will be taking everything I've learned from you back to the Council with the strong suggestion we implement it immediately. But…" she raised her head and glared at me, "… if you ever breath so much as a word about what happened here tonight. If you even hint at my submission to a human male, or to you… especially to you… I will make your life unbearable, do you understand?"

"Oh, honey, in this business we don't tell tales, and we certainly don't embarrass people for their sexual desires, so you have no need to worry." I ran a finger over her lips and trailed it down her breastbone to her nipple. "But you aren't leaving until tomorrow, so you may as well make the most of your time here. Now how about you get comfortable, and I'll show you just how skilled my tongue is?"

I didn't wait for her answer as I knew what it would be, and I shuffled down the bed and drew her legs apart. Her pussy was already wet and ready, and her clit stood to attention awaiting my touch. I lowered my head and smiled at the thought of what the rest of the night would bring as my tongue lapped at her opening.

Hi.
I'm Anna Heaven, and I just wanted to thank you for taking the time to read my book.
If you enjoyed it, please can I ask you to leave a review, as not only will it help me as an indie author, but I'd love to see what you have to say.
And if you want to know when my next book is available, you can subscribe to my Amazon author page in the USA or the UK, or you can connect with me on TWITTER as @HeavenErotica or FACEBOOK as AuthorAnnaHeaven. You can also sign up to my NEWSLETTER at https://annaheavenerotica.wordpress.com/newsletter/ for information about my books, sneak previews, competitions, and musings.
I'd love to connect with you!
Anna
xxx

Carry on reading for a preview of one of my other books, and information about my current box sets.

Melissa :

Melissa's first time with the Man of the House wasn't planned. It was her twenty-first birthday and she was out celebrating with her friend Chloe. When they returned, the man of the house wasn't happy, but that soon turned around, and all three were about to have a night to remember.

Candice:

Candice had never thought of The Man of the House in that way before. When he called to invite her to his cabin for the weekend, she thought he simply wanted to cheer her up after seeing her social media post about still being a virgin at eighteen. But he had other plans, and she was about to find out that the man she'd always loved was about to become everything she desperately needed.

Brandy:

Brandy didn't want The Man of the House to see her in the same light as her mother, so she took a job stripping to pay her own way through college. While she always worried about someone finding out what she did, she never expected her stepfather to turn up to one of her shows, and when he did, it turn her whole world on its head.

It was my twenty-first birthday and I'd gone out with friends. There were a few of us with birthdays around the same time so we decided to have a big school-themed bash.

I spent the afternoon getting ready with my best friend, Chloe, who I met at private school. We had a few glasses of Prosecco and put on some cheesy high school anthems to dance around to just to set the mood.

We'd both dug out our old school uniforms and were amazed to find we could still get into them, but as we were twenty-one not teenagers we decided to sex them up a bit.

Chloe opted for the full cheerleader outfit - being head-cheerleader back in school it was an obvious choice - and I slipped my school skirt and shirt over a sexy white lace bra and panties set. I switched out socks for white hold-up stockings, and added a pair of three inch black stilettos to create the look. Then I rolled up my skirt to my thighs and tied the front of my shirt in a knot so it would show off my slim waist. Finally I undid most of the buttons on my shirt to reveal my bra and cleavage, and put my hair up in high, childish pigtails.

"Damn, girl, even I'd fuck you looking like that," Chloe said as I did a twirl in front of her and placed a finger on the side of my lips in a coquettish smile.

'Chloe, you'd fuck anyone at any time," I said, laughing.

"I'm being serious! Don't you think I would?" Chloe raised her eyebrow and gave me a look that said, 'go on, dare me,' and I just had to.

She had her tongue down my throat and her hand in my pants when Mark, my stepdad, walked in.

I was so lost in what Chloe was doing to my pussy I didn't even notice he was there until Chloe stopped kissing me and turned my head towards the door. He stood there for a moment without saying a word, and then he grabbed the handle and closed the door, leaving us alone again.

"Oh my God, not only do you have the hottest stepdad ever, but did you see? We just gave him a fucking hard-on!"

"No we didn't," I said, laughing to hide my embarrassment.

"We did. I saw it, and he's fucking packing some major equipment!"

I pushed her away and turned to the mirror. "Whatever. He's my dad."

Chloe joined me and grabbed the brightest red lipstick I had. "And what? He's not your blood. Are you really going to tell me you haven't had at least one dirty dream about him? I know I have. He might be old, but he's hot as fuck, and I'd do him in a heartbeat."

"No, of course not!" I tried to turn away to hide the reddening of my cheeks but she pulled me back so I had no choice but to look at her.

"You have, you dirty slut. You've been fantasy-fucking your dad!"

There was no way Chloe was going to drop this, so I grinned and nodded, and punched her in the arm when she squealed with excitement.

"So, was he good? What did you do? Did you come?"

"Christ, Chloe, it was a dream. Does it matter?" I pushed her out of the way to get to the mirror and applied mascara to my lashes.

"I guess not," she said as she ran a glossy top-coat over her lips, "but you dream-fucked your dad. That is so fucking hot! Have you ever thought of telling him?"

"Jesus! No! He's married to my mum."

"And? It's not as if she has any time for him. Where is she right now? Off on another of her spirituality road trips? I bet Mark hasn't had any in months. I bet he'd fuck you in a heart-beat. Oh my God, I bet he wanks himself off every night at the thought of you giving him a blow job."

"That's just wrong," I said, laughing, and it was. He'd fucked my mother, was still fucking her when she was around. But I had to admit, even if it was only to myself, that I wanted him. For a man in his forties, he was seriously hot. He swam, cycled, and spent a couple of days at the gym, and he was fitter than most guys my age, and he had the most gorgeous blue eyes and a cheeky grin that made him look at least ten years younger.

Chloe was right. He might be married to my mum, and I might have called him Daddy for the past eighteen years, but if he came on to me, I'd do him in a heartbeat.

By the time we left for our night out we were in full party mode. Chloe was singing some boy band ballad at the top of her lungs to the uber driver and I was checking my phone to see who was already there.

The driver kept glancing at us in his mirror, and after paying the fare, I gave him a quick flash of my boobs as we were getting out of the car to brighten up his night.

"I saw that," Chloe said as we made our way into the club. "You should have flashed Mark like that before we left. Given him something to think about while he's all alone. It could have gotten him in the mood for when you get home."

"Please stop," I said as I pushed her towards the private room in the back of the club, but my mind was already playing over what would have happened if I had. Would he have shouted at me for acting completely inappropriately, or would he have shaken his head and laughed it off? Or... maybe he would have spanked me for being so naughty before pulling my pants down and... I pushed the thought out of my head, but it was too late. I was already turned on by the idea and I could feel my panties getting damp.

The rest of the evening was spent dancing, drinking and play-flirting with friends. Kyle, one of my old classmates, tried and failed to get me to give him a lap dance, and Sarah, who'd been out of the closet since seventh grade, managed to pull three different girls before disappearing into the bathroom with a fourth and not being seen again.

By the end of the night I was tipsy and ready to party some more, but the others were ready to call it a night.

Chloe appeared after being gone for the last hour with Jason, another former classmate and a Notre Dame Football scholarship student, looking flushed and rather agitated.

"Can you believe it," she said, showing me her phone. "Mother has locked the doors and gone to bed. I guess I'm staying at yours tonight." She put her arm around my shoulder as we walked out of the club. "But we could stop at the 7-eleven and pick up a couple of bottles to take home with us to carry on the night if you fancy it."

So that's what we did.

After giving yet another uber driver an eyeful in return for stopping off at the store, it was after midnight when we got back to the house, and we made our way to the kitchen to grab some glasses.

Chloe turned on some music as I dropped some ice into the tumblers and topped them up with vodka and soda. She grabbed me from behind and twirled me around the kitchen, her laugh drowning out the sound of the radio.

"You look so hot today. Dance with me," she said as she wrapped her arms around my waist.

I wasn't really into women, but Chloe was different. She was sexy and confident and fun, and the times we'd messed about were just that - messing about without all the awkward stuff, and forgotten about straight after. I moved in closer and kissed her, and she let go of my waist to undo the buttons on my shirt. I leaned back as her lips moved down my neck and across my chest, kissing around the outline of my bra.

"Melissa, can you turn the music down. It's late and I…"

Mark walked into the kitchen and stopped, staring at us. I pushed Chloe away and pulled my shirt closed. I tried to avoid eye contact with him, but in doing so I was drawn instead to the bulge in his jeans. Chloe was right. He did have a hard on seeing us together, and a sudden thrilling shiver ran down my back.

AVAILABLE IN PRINT FROM AMAZON

ALSO BY ANNA HEAVEN

TABOO DADDY CONFESSIONS 2:

AIMEE, HEATHER AND AMBER

Aimee:
When Aimee found herself locked out of the house, she didn't expect to find The Man of the House in his office watching home movies of her. Was he just reminiscing, or did he love her the same way she loved him? Aimee was determined to find out, and when she did, their relationship would never be the same again.

Heather:

The Man of the House, Scott, is a talented glamour photographer and a tough boss who demands efficiency, so when the model for a men's magazine shoot cancels at the last minute, Heather offers to take her place.
Will The Man of the House allow her to undertake such a sexy job, and will he be able to control himself?
With the temperature rising in the studio, Scott and Heather spend an afternoon together than will change their relationship forever.

Amber:

Amber is quite excited for The Man of the House to see her in her job as a flight attendant, but when the plane gets grounded, they find themselves in the position of having to share a hotel room. Will Amber be able to keep her hands to herself, or does Ryan feel the same way about her as she does about him?

AVAILABLE IN PRINT FROM AMAZON

Daddy's Little Darling:
The Man of the House thinks I'm dirty, but I've never been touched.
Truth is, I've only really had eyes for him. And it turns out he's had eyes for me too...
And he's about to claim me.

Daddy's Little Precious:

It's been a month since The Man of the House claimed me, and I'm super excited and nervous about this weekend's plan. Will they bring us closer together? And will I be able to take what he is offering?
I guess I'll find out.

Daddy's Little Treasure:
The Man of the House left me a list of tasks that I have to stick to because I am his now.
But will I be able to perform the way he wants me to? And what will happen to me if I don't?
I guess I'll find out.

AVAILABLE IN PRINT FROM AMAZON

www.ingramcontent.com/pod-product-compliance
Lightning Source LLC
Chambersburg PA
CBHW061250120726
48001CB00001B/243